me,
just different

me, just different

the reinvention of skylar hoyt

STEPHANIE MORRILL

a division of Baker Publishing Group
Grand Rapids, Michigan

Published by Revell
a division of Baker Publishing Group
P.O. Box 6287, Grand Rapids, MI 49516-6287
www.revellbooks.com

Printed in the United States of America

Library of Congress Cataloging-in-Publication Data
Morrill, Stephanie.
Me, just different / Stephanie Morrill.
p. cm. — (the reinvention of Skylar Hoyt ; bk. 1)
Summary: An incident at a summer party and major family crises have high school senior Skylar Hoyt rethinking her way of life, and with the help of a new boy at school and a youth coach at church, she begins to find her true self.
ISBN 978-0-8007-3377-3 (pbk.)
[1. Self-perception—Fiction. 2. Dating (Social customs)—Fiction. 3. Family problems—Fiction. 4. Popularity—Fiction. 5. High schools—Fiction. 6. Schools—Fiction. 7. Christian life—Fiction.] I. Title.
PZ7.M827215Me 2009
[Fic]—dc22 2009005111

For Ben. You always believed.

1

I wanted to refuse Eli, but I couldn't after the night we'd had.

At the snap of the gas pump, he pulled back from the kiss and looked into my eyes, awaiting my reaction. If my giving in surprised him, it didn't show. He smiled, and instead of saying what I already knew—that getting together was a mistake—I forced myself to smile back. Just like that, I became Eli's girlfriend.

"You should come to the game tonight," Eli said, unhooking the nozzle from the Land Rover's ever-thirsty tank. If he didn't have a gas guzzler, I couldn't help bemoaning, the kiss might never have happened.

"Skylar, did you hear me?"

I ordered my mind to return to our conversation. "Sorry. Lisa and I already talked about it. We'll be there."

Eli's eyebrow quirked with amusement. "She and John must be 'on' this week."

"Who can keep track anymore?"

He ripped his receipt from the kiosk and then surveyed my face. "I don't want us to be like that."

Now Eli seemed nervous, like he knew he'd served me another chance to back out. Jodi's face danced before my eyes, but last night's blur of frightening events trumped the promise I made her three years ago. Last night Eli was the only secure object, the only reason I'd woken up this morning with everything still intact.

I'd been confused, of course, to wake up in the back of Eli's new car. I'd sat up, my head killing me. I found Eli sleeping in the fully reclined driver's seat, his mouth hanging open, his breathing loud. I could remember only bits and pieces of how I'd come to be there, but I recalled enough to know one thing—I owed him for the night before.

But what a horrible reason to become his girlfriend now.

I opened my mouth, fully intending to back out, but when I looked at him, at those dark blue eyes, I couldn't do it. Would it really be so bad to date Eli Welling? We'd been friends for years and probably would have gotten together before now if Jodi wasn't in the picture. And he'd taken such good care of me last night.

I sucked in a deep breath. "Don't worry. We won't be like them."

Eli's mouth broadened with his dimpled smile, the one that made all the girls at school swoon, and we continued on our way.

A block from my house, Eli slowed the car alongside the curb. "Here okay? I mean, I'd walk you to the door if I could, but—"

"I know." I reached for the door handle but didn't leave. "Thanks again for last night. If you hadn't come in . . ." I didn't bother finishing. We both knew what might have happened if Eli's jealousy hadn't made him follow Aaron and me upstairs. "I want you to know it won't happen again."

"I know."

"Last night was a wake-up call for me." I fingered the buckle of my purse. I bought it yesterday because it matched one of my back-to-school outfits perfectly. It seemed important at the time, but now I didn't care. "I haven't been living the way I'm supposed to."

"You can't blame yourself for what Aaron did," Eli said.

"But I shouldn't have put myself in that position. I need to make some changes. Quit smoking, quit partying. Maybe go back to church." Despite the lack of thought I'd put into this, it made sense.

"I'll help." Eli reached for my hand. "I'll go to church with you."

"Really?" Our families went to the same church, but neither of us had gone since turning sixteen. That he'd go for me . . . "You'd do that?"

He shrugged. "Sure. I'll make my mom and you happy all at once. Everybody wins."

"That means a lot to me," I said, and rewarded him with my first real smile of the morning.

"See you tonight," he said as I climbed out.

"Oh—" I turned to face him. "You're not going to tell anyone about . . ."

He shook his head. "It's between you and me."

And as he drove away, I thought I might actually be happy about him blindsiding me with that kiss at the Quik-Trip service station.

It turned out Eli could've walked me to my door because only my younger sister was home. I heard her snoring through the pocket door dividing her bedroom and our bathroom. Had she been at the party last night? I cringed at the thought. I didn't fear Abbie tattling to Mom and Dad, but the idea of her seeing me there . . . I shivered and stepped into a steaming shower.

After scrubbing away the stench of keg party, I collapsed on my bed and stared at my cell phone. I knew I should call Jodi and tell her about Eli and me before word got around, but still I didn't dial her number. I didn't want to call my best friend and confess to be with her ex-boyfriend, the one guy who, out of respect for her, I'd sworn never to date.

But that wasn't the only reason Eli and I remained "just friends" all these years. I'd never felt anything stronger than friendship for him, though I didn't know why. Eli was everything I should have wanted—gorgeous, popular, athletic. If I couldn't fall in love with him, who could I fall in love with?

Lisa laughed when I arrived at the baseball fields. "What are you wearing?" She dropped her cigarette and stubbed it out with the heel of her espadrille.

I looked at my clothes—a white tank top and cutoffs. "What's wrong with what I'm wearing?"

"It's just so . . ." She waved her hand about, as if hoping to conjure the perfect word. "I don't know. Sneakers?"

"I walked here."

"But a white shirt and jeans? It's so not Skylar."

"I like to keep everyone on their toes," I said, but truthfully, I lacked the energy for one of my normal complicated ensembles.

Lisa linked our arms as we walked through the crowd. "Speaking of which, I hear you and a certain someone finally made it official."

I couldn't keep my voice from sounding panicked. "Who'd you hear that from?"

She blinked overdone eyes at me, my reaction apparently confusing her. "What do you mean? Jodi told me."

"You heard from Jodi?" Despite the intense humidity of the July night, goose bumps raised on my arms.

"You didn't tell her?"

"I didn't have a chance yet." I assumed Lisa would never point out the weakness of this excuse. I wanted to ask how Jodi sounded, but instead, I said, "Do you know who told her?"

"If it wasn't you, I'd guess Alexis."

"How did Alexis find out?"

Lisa shrugged. "How does Alexis ever know the things she does?"

I reached inside my purse before remembering I'd flushed my cigarettes down the toilet before leaving. "I shouldn't have quit smoking today."

"You quit? Why?"

"It's so bad for you," I said as we settled onto the metal bleachers. "Anyone who starts smoking these days is an idiot."

Lisa didn't answer right away, just chewed on her lower lip. "It's awful expensive, I guess."

From the team bench, Eli noticed us and waved, then turned his attention back to the game.

"I can't believe you two are together," Lisa said. "It's great. Now John and I have another couple to do stuff with."

"Like what stuff?"

"You know, couple stuff. Movies. Concerts. Dinner."

"We do that stuff now."

"Yeah, but it'll be different."

I frowned. That's what I was afraid of.

"So what did it?" Lisa asked.

"Did what?"

"Why'd you finally give in? I mean, Eli's been after you since we were freshmen, and you've always said there was no way. What changed?"

How could I tell her the truth? I didn't want my behavior last night, so naive, to be privy to my friends. Yet, if I omitted the intimate details, I couldn't think of a good explanation for my giving in to Eli.

So I gave Lisa a coy smile and said, "Well, that was before he got the Land Rover."

Lisa laughed, like I knew she would, but her giggles died a sudden death when Jodi appeared at the base of the bleachers.

One time Jodi dumped an entire soda on a boyfriend when she caught him cuddling in the food court with not-her. She punched, actually *punched,* Madison Embry when she overheard her bragging about hooking up with Alexis's first boyfriend. And at a party last summer, when rumors started flying about Sarah Humphrey and Jodi's boyfriend, Jodi waited for Sarah to pass out and then cut off her ponytail.

With all this running through my mind, I could barely utter, "Hey."

"I hear you have big news," Jodi said, masked in her poker face.

"Uh . . ."

She mounted the bleachers and took her normal spot in life, my right side. "You know, Eli's my ex-boyfriend."

"Um, I do," I said. Lisa shifted away from me.

Jodi pulled an opened bag of peanut M&M's from her purse. "Want one?"

I peeked inside, then shook my head.

Jodi burst into laughter. "Relax, Skylar. You're acting like I poisoned them or something." She bumped her shoulder against mine. "I'm fine with you and Eli."

"You are?" I expected to feel relief, but none came.

"Sure," she said, tossing back a handful of candy. "Not like it's a big shock."

"Eli's batting," Lisa said.

Jodi shook more candy into her palm. "If I were a guy, I think I'd play soccer. I wouldn't want to wear those tight pants."

Who was this girl making casual conversation about the pitfalls of baseball pants? I'd encountered her nasty temper many times since we'd met in eighth grade. Her support of Eli and me seemed worse than if she'd bawled me out in front of everybody.

"Do you know if Alexis is coming?" Lisa asked as Eli fouled off the first pitch.

Jodi shook her head. "She doesn't get off work until after the game."

Lisa accepted the M&M's Jodi offered. "I'd hate to have to work. It spoils the summer."

"Are we meeting up with her later?" I asked.

"I told her Lisa, John, and I would be available," Jodi said, "but you and Eli probably wanted to be alone. New love and all."

I opened my mouth to respond, not sure what I intended to say, but Eli interrupted me by grounding one past the short stop. I cheered the same as always, shouting and clapping, but Eli did something new. First base secured, he tipped his hat at me, causing the other spectators, mostly parents, to turn and look.

"Hey, Romeo, keep your head in the game!" his coach said.

"Knock it off," I said to my two cackling friends.

"Oh, Skylar, he's just so proud you're finally his girlfriend, he can't help it." Jodi stood. "I need Red Vines. You two want anything?"

Lisa shook her head. "Won't we go to Sheridan's afterward?" We'd haunted Sheridan's Frozen Custard all summer long.

Jodi smiled, big and humorless. "Tonight is a special occasion." She marched down the bleachers to the concession stand.

Lisa and I followed her with our eyes. "I can't believe how well she's taking it," Lisa said. "I mean, she doesn't seem mad at all."

"I wish she'd just yell at me," I said.

"You're crazy." Our conversation paused briefly as John doubled. Lisa clapped and whistled. "You know Jodi's not one to hide her feelings. Remember what happened to Sarah Humphrey when Jodi suspected she'd been flirting with Trent? If Jodi was actually mad, she'd have snuck up from behind and cut off your ponytail or something."

"I hope you're right." But I couldn't shake my fears of her calm exterior eventually giving way to something worse than a spiteful haircut.

After the game, Eli apologized for embarrassing me. "I guess I wasn't thinking," he said, wiping sweat from his forehead.

"It'd have been fine except Jodi's here."

He glanced at her chatting away with Lisa and John. "How bad?"

"It's hard to put it into words."

He gave me a once-over. "No black eyes, and you're still wearing the clothes you showed up in." He tilted my head to see the back. "Hair isn't shorter."

"It's not funny. She's acting really, really weird. Like she's totally okay with us."

Eli shrugged. "Maybe she is. Jodi and I have been over for years. Maybe she really doesn't care."

"It's official," I said. "You know nothing about girls."

Eli laughed. "I'll use the bathroom and then we'll go, okay?"

I considered joining Jodi and Lisa, who stood near the team bench giggling over something John said, but instead, I stood there with Eli's bat bag at my feet. Maybe he wouldn't mind dropping me off at home. Spending an entire night with my friends sounded exhausting. What a big difference twenty-four hours could make. This time last night, I'd not only been one of them, I'd been something like the leader of the group. Now going for ice cream seemed like a terrible chore.

I emerged from my thoughts to find a strange guy standing in front of me, grinning like we knew each other. "You Skylar?"

He wore the same uniform as Eli, but I didn't recognize him. I took a step back. "Yeah."

His smile widened. "Connor Ross. Nice to meet you." He grabbed my hand, as if our parents stood nearby grading this exchange, and gave it several enthusiastic pumps. "Eli's giving me a ride home. Normally I don't need one, my parents bring me, but all my brothers are sick and—" He interrupted himself with a laugh. "Well, it's a long story."

"Hmm." I looked beyond him, trying to send my friends an SOS with my brain waves. No luck.

Connor removed his baseball hat to scratch at his coarse, damp hair. "Eli said dropping me off wouldn't be a problem because you and I live by each other. What street are you on?"

He looked like a nice enough guy, but so had Aaron. I intended to remember how impossible it is to distinguish the nice ones from the bad. "Aberdeen," I lied, glancing at the men's bathroom. How could Eli have left me alone out here? I needed him.

John, Lisa, and Jodi sauntered past us on their way to the parking lot. "See you there, Skylar!" Lisa said.

I yearned to join them. I wanted to be anywhere but standing here making small talk with a strange guy, but it would be rude to run after them. I could only wave and envy their retreat.

Connor watched the lucky three slip into the crowd. "You know Lisa Rivers?"

"Yeah." I sighed. My opportunity for escape had come and gone.

"What's her deal? Half the time she's hanging all over

John, but otherwise she flirts with anything male that moves. Last week it was my fifteen-year-old brother."

I caught myself smiling. "That's Lisa."

"She was so aggressive I told Chris to be careful with his drink." Connor chuckled. "I was afraid she'd slip something in it."

My mouth filled with bitterness, as if I could taste my dislike for him. "You shouldn't make jokes like that."

He stopped laughing. "I didn't mean anything by it."

I took a step away from him, ready to leave and no longer caring how rude I might appear, when Eli materialized. "Oh good, you found each other. Skylar, I told Connor I'd give him a lift home. He lives just down the street from you." He snapped his fingers as he realized the flaw in this plan. "Although I'm not taking Skylar home. We're going out for ice cream with some friends. You been to Sheridan's, Connor?"

"No."

"Best place in town. You have to come." Eli draped his arm around me as we walked, despite having just finished nine innings of baseball. "That way you'll know some more people before school starts. Of course you already know John and my girl, Skylar . . ."

I faded away from them, disinterested in anything they might have to say. Instead, I thought about having Eli all over me while Jodi watched. I half wished she'd dumped her Diet Coke over my head while we sat in the bleachers. It seemed torturous to postpone the fight. Maybe that was her intent.

When we reached Eli's car, I gaped at Connor as he went for shotgun. What kind of moocher bummed a ride, then assumed the front seat over the girlfriend?

"Skylar," Connor said as I yanked at the backdoor handle. He held open the passenger door. "I was getting this for you."

"Oh." I tried to smile, but failed. "Thanks."

He offered his hand, helping me climb into the vehicle. "I'd never hitch a ride and take the front seat. Especially from a girl."

"Some guys would," I said, buckling my seat belt.

"True," Connor said. "And you never can tell."

Didn't I know it.

"You're not trying to steal my girl, are you?" Eli called to the backseat. While he sounded flippant, I caught the flash of jealousy in his eyes. An endearing quality when I needed rescuing, but annoying when it spilled into Connor's and my casual moment of friendliness. As if I would ever be interested in a guy like Connor.

Sheridan's Frozen Custard sat close to the busy road, its lights bright and beckoning amid the row of dark storefronts. This late at night and this deep in the summer, teenagers dominated the parking lot and spilled onto the grass, drunk on sugar and twilight.

By the time we arrived, Alexis already sat in the bed of John's F-150, gorging on a large cup of custard.

"Yay, Skylar's here," Alexis said as we approached.

Eli leaned against the truck. "What about me?"

She shrugged and smiled flirtatiously. Alexis did everything flirtatiously.

Connor stuck out his hand. "I'm Connor."

Alexis looked at it for a moment, appearing as stunned as I'd been, then offered hers in return. "Alexis."

"Nice to meet you," he said.

Eli's fingertips fell soft on my neck. "What do you want, Skylar?"

"I need to look at the menu." I adjusted my ponytail, forcing him to move his hand.

He didn't seem to notice, just smiled and smoothed my hair. "Connor, you want anything?"

"Nah, I'm good," he said, positioning himself beside Alexis. As we walked away, I heard her draw him into conversation. While Connor likely interpreted this as friendly, all of us knew Alexis was a huge gossip. She wanted first dibs on whatever dirt Connor had to offer.

"What's with that guy?" I asked Eli, tone sharper than intended.

"Connor? He comes on a little strong, but don't worry. He's real nice." Eli combed through the ends of my ponytail, fingers catching on a knot. "You wouldn't know it from looking at him, but he's a power hitter."

"Well, I don't like him." My stomach itched and my mouth tasted bitter again. Why did we have to invite someone new out with our group, tonight of all nights? I wasn't ready for new guys just yet. "He's just . . . I don't know. He makes me uncomfortable."

"You have no reason to be worried," Eli said, then planted an awkward kiss on my cheek.

Okay, ew. Did everything with us have to be so serious relationship-y? Why must even the simple act of walking from the parking lot to the ice cream line convey our couple status to the world? Especially with Jodi here.

When we joined Jodi in line, I thought Eli hanging all over me would prompt her death glare, but instead, she looked at us with desperation. "These two are driving me crazy." She nodded at John and Lisa, who stood in front of her absorbed in some gushy conversation. It involved a lot of nuzzling and, "No, *you* are."

"Next," the Sheridan's employee called from the window. This meant John and Lisa, but they didn't notice. "Next!"

Jodi flicked the back of Lisa's head. "That's you."

"Oh!" Lisa said with a giggle.

Jodi rolled her eyes, but a moment later, her mouth drooped. "I want a boyfriend."

I suppose Connor happened to be at the right place at the right time. Why else would Jodi attach herself to him the moment we returned to the truck? His height, freckles, and constant grin reminded me of a pesky little brother. On nights Jodi behaved like herself, she liked her guys tall, blond, and worthy of a contract with Abercrombie and Fitch, like Eli. Obviously, desperation caused this.

"He's adorable," she confided to me in our moment of privacy en route to the trash can. "Did you see him reading my palm? He says I'm going to have a long and happy life."

She sounded like she wanted to have a long and happy life *with Connor*.

"We just met him, Jo," I said. "You should be careful."

"Connor's harmless," she said, and I must admit it appeared she was right. He wasn't like Aaron, so smooth and charming. Connor was the opposite, all chatter and awkward angles.

"You can do way better," I said as we sidestepped a couple of cackling girls.

"I guess I could." She pitched her cup toward the trash can. It hit the rim but bounced in anyway. "So. You and Eli are cute together."

My mouth went dry, and I double-checked to make sure she wasn't holding scissors or a soda or anything. "If it bothers you, I'll end things with him."

She waved this idea away. "Completely unnecessary."

"But I always told you I wouldn't date him."

"I know, but I expected it would happen someday."

This made me feel even worse. "Eli and I are no big deal," I said.

Jodi fixed her eyes on Connor as we started back to the truck. "You really don't think I should like Connor?"

I looped my arm through hers, overcome with guilt. "Like whoever you want."

2

"Abbie?" Mom called when I returned home that evening.

"No, it's me." I walked through the entry, making myself visible.

Mom sat posed on the white couch. Even with her loose ponytail and makeup-free skin, she appeared to be in the midst of a photo shoot. "The Modern Homemaker," the description might read.

"Abbie isn't home yet?" I asked.

"Take off your shoes, Skylar." She turned the page of her catalog—Williams-Sonoma, though it had been months since she cooked anything more complicated than frozen lasagna.

I slipped out of my sandals. "Abbie isn't home?"

"It's just a few minutes after."

I glanced at the clock. "It's thirty-four minutes after."

Mom offered no reply. She held up the page to me and tapped the picture of Le Creuset pans. "Do you think the blue ones would match our kitchen?"

"Do pans need to match the decor?"

"If we hang them from a rack over the island they do."

I looked through the kitchen to the French doors of Dad's

office. His desk light burned even at this late hour. When I turned back to Mom, I found her awaiting my answer about the pans. "It's hard to tell from a catalog."

"Hmm," Mom said. "Maybe tomorrow I'll go to the store."

My cell phone hollered from my bag. I suspected it was Eli, who'd taken to obsessive calling now that we were official. Instead, Abbie's cell number flashed on the screen. My stomach churned because Abbie only called me for one reason.

"It's Jodi," I said, excusing myself. I answered the call but said nothing else until I reached my bedroom. Despite both the stairs and my closed door, I whispered, "Tell me this isn't what I think it is."

"Can you come get me?" Abbie asked.

I sighed. "No chance you're at Jenna's?"

"Would I call you if I was?"

I hung up without answering.

Downstairs, I snatched my bag from the floor. "I need to pick up Jodi. She was on a date with this guy, and they had a fight. He left her at the movie theater."

Mom wagged her head. "This is why high school is way too young to start dating. You're not emotionally prepared to handle situations like this."

Mom was loose when it came to curfews and how we dressed, but she never budged about boys. We could have guy friends and hang out in large groups, but we weren't allowed to date until college.

"Would you mind stopping by Jenna's?" she asked as I tugged on my shoes. "Abbie's over there, and I'm sure she's lost track of time again."

"Sure. I'll be back soon."

Mom responded with the turning of a page.

When I pulled up to Lance's house—a common occurrence these last six months—Abbie waited on his porch rather than at his window. In exchange for my picking her up, Abbie cleaned our bathroom and paid for my gas. Before last night, this seemed like a great trade, but now my conscience nagged at me. What kind of older sister was I?

Abbie eased into the front seat. "Thanks, Skylar."

I didn't answer, just pulled away from the curb. From the corner of my eye, I watched her attempts to finger-comb her long, tousled hair. "There's a brush in my bag," I said.

"Great, thanks."

This wasn't how our parents raised us. They brought us up in the church and beat into us that sex was for marriage only, long before we even knew what that meant. I couldn't be sure about the progression of Abbie and Lance's relationship, but I wasn't stupid enough to think they were just playing Scrabble in his bedroom.

I cleared my throat. "This is the last time I'll be able to pick you up."

Abbie stopped brushing midstroke and looked at me, her cinnamon eyes big and beautiful. "Why?"

"I just can't do this anymore," I said, finding my hands suddenly slippery on the steering wheel. These weren't the kinds of conversations Abbie and I had. "It's not right, what you and Lance are doing, and you know that. As your big sister, I can't encourage this kind of behavior."

Abbie erupted with amused laughter. "I'm sorry, but weren't you out all last night at Jodi's party? And a few nights before that, didn't you come home so drunk it's a miracle you didn't wake up Mom and Dad? And two weeks ago wasn't it you who—"

"I know I haven't been the best role model," I said. "But things have changed. I'm not doing that stuff anymore."

Abbie rolled her eyes. "Please, Skylar. Both of us know you'll be back to partying in a week."

I sucked in a long breath and released it. "All I'm saying is I'm no longer picking you up at Lance's when Mom thinks you're at Jenna's."

Abbie harrumphed at this. She didn't say another word to me the rest of the night.

"Do you have Connor's number?" Jodi asked as we relaxed poolside at the country club a couple days later.

I propped myself onto my elbows so I could see her full face. "Connor *Ross*?"

"What other Connor do we know?" Dark sunglasses hid her eyes, but I could tell she rolled them. "Does Eli have his number?"

I hesitated. "I'm sure there's a team contact list of some kind."

"Could you ask him for it?"

"Jodi . . ."

"What's the big deal? I know you two talk a zillion times a day."

I'd hoped Jodi's interest in Connor would be like one of her signature crushes, lasting a single night before evaporating. Then Connor would become what countless other guys had before him—something we all laughed about the next morning. Jodi would say to me, "Please don't tell anybody I even considered liking him," and Connor would fade into an inside joke, then someone neither of us remembered. But for reasons mysterious to me, Connor had more staying power than his predecessors.

I waved at the crowded pool. "This place is crawling with good-looking guys. Even a few you haven't dated."

Jodi gave me a look. "Ha ha."

"Seriously. See the guy by the vending machines? He's been watching you for the last fifteen minutes."

She laughed. "He's watching you."

"No he isn't."

"I'm looking at him right now and we're not making eye contact. He's looking at you."

I lowered my sunglasses—yep, she was right.

"Well, forget about him," I said, pushing my glasses back into place. "My point is, if you're looking for an end-of-summer boyfriend, Connor isn't the only option."

At the sound of his name, her mouth curled into a smile. "What's wrong with Connor? He's so sweet. I've never dated anybody sweet." She sighed, lovesick, and rolled onto her flat stomach. "Do you think he likes me?"

I looked at my best friend, tan and blonde. "What's not to like?"

Jodi smiled and then drifted to sleep in the sunshine.

When I returned home, hair stiff and smelling of chlorine, I found Mom on her way out.

"Oh, hi," she said, stopping at the sight of me. "I didn't expect you home so soon."

"Jodi had to work. Where are you going?"

"Counseling."

"I thought your marital counseling was on Tuesdays." I flipped through the mail. Only credit card offers and college brochures came to me, but still I checked every day in case of something exciting, like an anonymous love letter.

"We changed it to Thursdays," Mom said, smoothing the skirt of her summer dress. "Well, I need to go or I'll be late. Wake your sister up, okay?"

After she left, I trotted upstairs and peeked into Abbie's room. Beams of sunshine sliced across her face, but she slept undisturbed. "Wake up," I said from the doorway.

She blinked in the glory of the afternoon. "What time is it?" The first words she'd spoken to me since our fight nearly thirty-six hours ago.

"Almost one. Get up. I'm making lunch."

Abbie groaned. "Please, no more tuna salad."

"Well, Mom hasn't bought groceries this week, so there's not much else."

"That's okay. I'm not hungry."

I raised my eyebrows. Abbie burned so much energy with all her Abbieness that she could eat around the clock and never gain an ounce. "You aren't hungry?"

"Nope," she said, and resettled into her pillow.

I frowned as her breathing deepened. Fine. What did I care if she slept the day away?

As I threw together a meager lunch, Jodi called. She tried to whisper, but her voice came out high and squeaky. "Guess who I have a date with tomorrow night."

"Tell me it's not Connor."

She seemed not to hear me. "You know how you always say if I like a guy, I should tell him instead of waiting around for him to ask me out? Well, I did. And he sounded happy about it!"

"Of course he did. Wouldn't you be happy if Brad Pitt called and asked you for a date?"

Jodi considered this. "Isn't he a little old for me?"

"Do you get my point or not?" I asked, licking mayonnaise from my finger.

"I thought you'd be proud of me for making the first move. It's scary."

"I am proud, but I don't think—" I realized something. "Hey, how did you get his number?"

A shrill voice interrupted. "Jodi, are you on the phone in there?"

"No," Jodi answered, and the line went dead.

How Jodi managed to stay employed at Gap longer than a month mystified me. Not only did she show up late for every shift, but I received tons of hushed calls from the storeroom regarding either an incredibly cute customer who'd asked for her number, or an incredibly annoying customer she'd told off. Management tolerated her sketchy work ethics because Jodi's sales rates were double those of any other floor employee, thanks to guys who bought stuff just to talk to her.

I carried my sad-looking sandwich outside. The family who had lived here before us sank a lot of money into making the backyard beautiful, with butterfly gardens and shrubs lining the fence. Now it was overgrown and underwatered. No one but us saw it, so why would Mom and Dad put effort into making it look nice?

I flopped onto one of the teak chaises. Senior year started in a month. I'd never been so ready. Every summer activity I'd anticipated—sleeping in, swimming, and gobs of time with my girlfriends—now left me too free to think of Aaron. Especially because my friends kept bringing him up.

"You guys were so flirty at the party, and then the next thing we knew you were with Eli. What's the deal?"

"He just wasn't my type," I said to each of them. The wobble in my voice seemed obvious to me, but no one ever noticed. "He was so clingy, it was just pathetic."

Why couldn't they just leave me alone? Had my friends always been so annoying? I'd never noticed before, but now they seemed so . . . cliché. Typical popular girls—only guys, clothes, and makeup occupied them. No uniqueness.

Aaron had agreed.

"You're different than your friends," he'd said, standing close. Flattered, I allowed him to lean in and kiss me.

Thinking about Aaron made my head swim, as if I were still in that room, the roofy just taking effect. I tried turning off the mental pictures but couldn't stop them.

That dark room. His handsome face so close to mine it blurred. The alarm clock blinking an incorrect time—it hadn't been reset from the power outage the night before.

I tipped my face toward the sun, hoping to remind the frozen place inside me that I was safe now. But still . . .

The weight of him. My dry mouth. My meager voice asking for a drink of water.

"I'm so sorry," I said, but I wasn't sure to whom. God, I supposed. "I didn't mean to."

The sticky smell of his cologne, his breath hot on my face.

I reached for my phone and pressed a random speed dial number. I didn't know who I called until Alexis answered.

"You busy?" I asked. "I'm thinking about hitting the mall."

3

Mom studied me as we ate dinner.

"You're making me nervous," I said through a mouthful of lasagna.

"You really want to go tonight?"

"Would you rather I not?"

"No, I'm just surprised. Pleasantly, of course, but surprised." She picked up her glass of iced tea but held it without drinking. "I can't remember when you last expressed an interest in youth group activities."

I shrugged. "It's my senior year. I don't want to miss out on anything."

"Since I'm only starting my sophomore year and I have plenty of youth group events in my future, can I skip tonight?" Abbie asked as she poked at the limp green beans on her plate.

Mom shot Abbie a silencing look and returned her attention to me. "I must say, it's so nice to have the entire family at church these days."

I'd been true to my word and hadn't missed a Sunday the last four weeks. Just getting dressed for church made me feel better about myself.

Abbie put on a big, fake smile. "It's delightful. Can I be excused?"

Mom blinked at Abbie as if trying to recognize a vaguely familiar face. "Sure."

"We leave in fifteen," I said.

"Can't wait," Abbie called over her shoulder.

Mom sighed as Abbie thundered up the stairs. "I don't know what to do with her. You were never like this at her age."

Heck, I'd been like her a month ago.

"She'll grow out of it."

Mom sighed again and pushed away her plate. "This isn't what I'm in the mood to eat. How about you?"

These days, Mom served lasagna so often I sometimes gagged at the smell of it. "Well . . ."

She went to the freezer—a stainless steel Viking delivered Wednesday, despite the other being only a few years old—and pulled out a half gallon of Rocky Road.

I salivated. "You're serious?"

"Before your father and I got married, I never ate a real dinner. I always had cereal or popcorn or something." She pulled a couple bowls from the cupboard and paused, thoughtful-like. "I miss those days."

"Speaking of Dad . . ." Now that I had her attention, I wasn't sure I wanted it. Mom and I didn't have real conversations, so why did I think I should bring up her and Dad? But I couldn't turn back now. "How's counseling going?"

Mom dropped my bowl in front of me, and for a moment, I thought she might yell. Mom could be like that, totally fine one minute and furious the next. No matter her mood, you knew the opposite lingered close below the surface, like she contained two different people.

But she didn't get mad. "We're not in counseling anymore," she said, her voice taking on a weary sound.

"Oh." Now even ice cream didn't sound good. "I thought it was going well."

She selected her words with care. "Your father isn't sure we're getting enough out of it to make it worth the investment. Counseling is expensive."

I wished I hadn't asked. There are things you'd rather believe about your parents, like they're happy, even if you know it's a long shot.

"I should get ready to go," I said.

Mom nodded. It looked as though she might have more to say, but she left it at, "Have a good time tonight."

In the car, Abbie seemed particularly moody. She answered my questions about music and air temperature with mild grunts as she stared out the window.

"Are you still mad at me?" I finally asked.

"No."

"I know what I said at Lance's might have been hard to hear, but it's been like four weeks now and—"

"I don't care," Abbie said, loud this time. "Lance broke up with me anyway."

"Oh." I wished for something smart to say, sage advice from the older sister, but I came up empty. "I'm sorry."

"It doesn't matter."

"Abbie, you guys were together for a long time. It's rough."

"You don't know what you're talking about"—she turned back to the window—"so just leave me alone, okay?"

I intended to until I glanced at the passenger mirror

and caught her restraining tears. When I gave her leg an awkward pat, she sobbed. I returned my hand to the wheel. "Breakups are hard. It's okay to be upset."

"I'm not upset about Lance," Abbie said, her words strangled with emotion. "I mean, I am, but not really."

"Then what's going on?"

She looked at me. "You can't tell anyone."

"Of course."

"And you can't be mad at me."

I stared at her for a dangerous amount of time, considering I was driving. When she trembled, I knew. "You're not . . . ?"

She bit her lip and nodded, then broke into fresh tears. "When I woke up this morning I felt awful. I knew even before I took the test."

"Is this why he broke up with you?" I asked, hands tightening on the wheel as if it were Lance's throat.

"No. That happened the night you picked me up," Abbie said with a weak smile. "That's why I looked so ragged when I came out. I'd been crying."

"Why did you let me lecture you? Why didn't you tell me?"

Abbie shrugged.

I turned into the church parking lot, my hands moving on their own because my brain contained only Abbie. When I parked, neither of us moved.

"So. What do you want to do?"

Abbie turned to me. "About what?"

"The baby, Abbie," I snapped.

Her eyes narrowed. "It's none of your business, okay? This is my problem and I'll decide what to do."

"Are you . . ."

"If you're thinking what I think you are, I'm insulted. I'd never—"

"No, not that. I meant, are you going to keep the baby or put it up for adoption?"

"Back off, okay? I haven't had time to think about it."

"I can help—"

"I don't want your help." She wrestled out of her tangled seat belt. "Your job is to keep your mouth shut." She slammed the car door.

In the rearview mirror, I watched her stalk across the parking lot, her long, copper ponytail swinging with each angry step. My head, heavy with guilt, fell to the steering wheel. I had driven her to Lance's knowing exactly what was going on, but as long as she ponied up for gas I hadn't cared.

I should pray. "God?" But I didn't know what to say next. What could I pray for in a situation like this? The baby already existed. Should I pray for how our parents would react? For what Abbie's life would be like after this?

I leaned back and wiped my eyes. If only I'd gotten my act together sooner, I might have been able to prevent this. If only she hadn't followed so closely in my footsteps when it came to partying. If only I could snap my fingers and make this all disappear.

I spotted Eli's Land Rover across the parking lot. I needed to head inside before he tired of waiting for me and left.

Climbing out of my car, I heard a chipper and unwelcome, "Hey."

Connor. He leaned against my trunk, casual-like, as if a month of hanging out with my friends made us buddies.

"What are you doing here?" I asked.

"I saw you sitting in your car. I thought I'd walk in with you."

My teeth ground with impatience. "I meant, what are you doing here at my church?"

"Oh, that. I go here. Didn't you see me this morning? I waved."

"No, I didn't."

"That's good. I thought you were ignoring me. It's nicer that you just didn't see me." Connor rocked onto his heels. "You heading in?"

"Yeah."

"So." He fell into step with me. "You doing okay?"

"Why?" I asked, cutting my eyes to him. What had he seen?

He shrugged. "It took you awhile to get out of the car. I thought something might be wrong."

"Nothing's wrong. I'm fine," I said, punching "fine."

"Okay." Connor left it at that.

When we walked in, I noticed Abbie first. She sat in a corner of the room, giggling with some friends. She looked young and silly, but I wouldn't say innocent. She possessed a quality, a maturity, that set her apart from the other girls her age. And I wasn't the only one who noticed. I often caught our parents watching her with wary eyes. Abbie's smart mouth, always working faster than her brain, and her untamed rebellious streak were neon signs reading, "Watch out—I could be trouble."

And here we were.

"Here you are," Eli said, leaning to kiss me. He came out of nowhere, and I reacted by pulling away. His face darkened. "What's wrong?"

"Nothing, I—I didn't realize it was you."

"Oh." He smiled. "Well, then I'm glad you pulled away." He looked beyond me to Connor. "I didn't know you went to church here."

"My family just started," Connor said. They shared a complicated handshake the baseball team had developed over the summer. Connor gestured to a guy lurking near the door. "This is my brother Chris. He's a sophomore."

Chris ducked his head, endearingly bashful, unlike his older brother.

"You're the same age as Skylar's sister," Eli said, pointing across the auditorium. "We'll introduce you."

"Who's your sister?" Connor asked, scanning the auditorium.

"There by the stereo. With the reddish hair."

"*That's* your sister?" Connor said, turning from Abbie to me as if he'd find a resemblance.

This reaction—a common one—didn't surprise me, but I never knew how to handle it. My mother was a native Hawaiian, and Dad was some confusing blend of European countries. When people as different looking as my parents had kids, you'd expect a mix of features. Not so with Abbie and me. I inherited everything of Mom's—her mocha skin, her thick, straight hair, even her cool manner—while Abbie sported Dad's fair skin and cinnamon eyes. The only things Abbie and I had in common were our last name and petite build.

I offered Connor the simplest explanation I knew. "I take after our mom, who's Hawaiian. Abbie looks like our dad."

"Babe, your eye makeup is runny," Eli said out of nowhere. Since when did he have pet names for me? "Have you been crying?"

"No." I wiped under my eyes with my fingertips. "I just had something in my contact earlier."

Before Connor could open his big mouth and tattle about me crying in the car, the youth coaches summoned us deeper into the auditorium. They had us compete in awful activities like playing softball with a balloon between our knees, followed by inner-tube sumo wrestling—their attempt at helping us bond. As I shimmied into the inner-tube, I couldn't help questioning how these stupid games could possibly make me into a better person. *That's* why I wanted to be at youth group.

After the games, we split into small groups to share prayer requests. Eli leaned close to me. "You're quiet tonight."

"Am I?" I said. "I don't know why."

"Eli, how can we pray for you this week?" Heather asked before Eli could push me any further.

Heather Silver had quickly become my favorite youth coach because she didn't force me to play the third game of the night, mummy wrap relays. (I'd been a decent sport about softball and wrestling, I thought.) Plus she had on a totally cute shirt. When I asked where she got it, dreading that her answer would be some generic store at the mall, she surprised me by saying she'd made it. Usually I bought my clothes at boutique-type places to avoid the embarrassment of showing up to a party wearing the same dress as four other girls, but if I could learn how to *make* my own clothes . . .

"Skylar?" Heather smiled at me. "Is there something we

can pray about for you?" She pressed her pen to her notebook, prepared to write down whatever words fell from my mouth. Clearly, Heather knew how to pray. Maybe she would even know how to pray for Abbie, but of course I didn't want to broadcast Abbie's pregnancy.

"No," I said.

She tipped her head, and I noticed her earrings, silver and wiry. Had she made those too? "Nothing?"

"Nope." I offered my most convincing smile.

"Okay. Connor?"

As Heather moved on, my conscience nagged at me. Was it like a double sin or something if you didn't pray and then lied about what you needed prayer for? Or did it even matter if I prayed? If God knew everything, didn't he know better than I did what I needed? Was it possible to insult him by asking for something wrong?

I tried easing my mind with this idea, that it might be better if I kept my mouth shut, but after the groups dispersed, I couldn't keep my eyes from trailing to Heather as she moved about the room helping clean up. I kept seeing her pen pressed to her notepad, waiting for me to share what I needed prayer for. Heather had expertise I needed.

"You okay?" Eli asked. I realized he'd been talking to me, but I hadn't heard a word.

"I'm fine," I said, pushing past him. "I'll be right back."

I caught Heather in the midst of a conversation with another youth coach. She stopped and smiled at me. "Hey, Skylar."

"Could I talk to you in private?" I asked with a nervous glance at the other adult.

"Sure," Heather said and tossed the trash she'd collected.

She took in the chaotic room. "How about back in the offices?"

I followed her through doors I hadn't previously noticed. Back here, with the cubicles and fake greenery, we could have been at my dad's office rather than church.

"What's on your mind?" Heather asked, leaning against the copier.

I caught myself fidgeting with the ends of my braids, and stuffed my hands into the pockets of my Bermuda shorts. "If I ask you to pray about something, it's in confidence, right? You don't, like, have to report it to Max or anything?"

Heather's forehead creased. "It depends. If it involves drugs, alcohol, abuse, or any other illegal activities, I'm obligated to pass it on. Otherwise, whatever you say to me stays between us."

I chewed on my lip for a moment. "Well, earlier when I said there wasn't anything I need prayer for, I wasn't being entirely truthful."

Heather nodded but didn't say anything.

"The thing is, there's a lot going on in my life right now, but none of it is really stuff I'm doing. It's family stuff."

"You can be as specific or vague as you'd like, Skylar."

I tried to work it out in my head first, general words suggesting there was "something" going on with my sister and my parents weren't really in the "position" to cope. Finally, I blurted, "Abbie's pregnant, and I don't think my parents' marriage is strong enough to handle it."

Heather tried hard to mask her surprise, but still it leaked through her eyes. "Oh. I . . ." She shook her head and tried again. "I'll certainly be praying for you and your family."

"Should I not have told you?" I asked as her stunned expression remained. "I'm kinda new to this religious stuff."

"It's fine to tell me." She offered a nice smile. "That's what I'm here for."

I released a breath of relief. "Okay, good. It just seemed like something that needed to be prayed about, but I don't know how to yet, and you clearly know what you're doing."

Heather chuckled. "I don't know if any of us ever feels like we know what we're doing when it comes to prayer." She scrawled something on a scrap of copier paper. "The only way to really screw up praying is by not doing it." She handed the paper to me. "This is my cell, and it's on all the time. Feel free to call whenever."

"Really?" I wouldn't want even my closest friends interrupting my sleep.

"Sure. I might not be too coherent if you call at three in the morning, but you're welcome to give it a try."

"I really appreciate this." My eyes tickled with tears and I trained my gaze on the floor.

Heather looked about to say something else, but the office door swung open and Max entered, a packet of paper in one hand. He smiled. "Hello, ladies. Connor still back here?"

My heart beat so loud, it seemed to thump in my head rather than my chest.

"I'm right here." Connor peeked out from one of the nearby cubicles, the one with Max's name stuck on the wall. The pitch of his voice rose, and he avoided eye contact. He'd heard the whole thing.

"Sorry it took me so long." Max handed the packet to

Connor with a jovial slap on the back. "Tell your dad he's welcome to fax or email this into the office."

"I will." Connor clicked his gaze to me.

"I have to go," I think I said. "Thanks, Heather."

"Skylar," Connor said, but I ignored him and pushed through the doors into the auditorium.

"Skylar," he said again, this time on my heels. "I'm so sorry. I didn't know what to do, I—"

"You could have spoken up." I whirled to face him and he bumped into me. "You shouldn't have just sat there eavesdropping."

Connor took a step back. "You're right. I'm sorry."

"I'll ruin you if you tell anyone. I mean it."

"I won't tell anyone."

"Not even Jodi. Swear to me," I said, my finger in his face.

He swallowed. "I promise."

"Good," I said. "And stay away from me."

With that, I turned and stalked away. Wasn't it enough Connor had somehow weaseled his way into Jodi's heart? I'd spent these last four weeks listening to her gush about their most recent date, and as if that wasn't enough, now he'd involved himself in my home life.

I found Abbie camped out by the exit door, arms over her chest and face cross. "Where have you been?" She noticed my face. "You look angry."

"Nothing important." Which was true, because my anger was about Connor.

I jabbed at the door, hoping for cool, fresh air. Instead, I got a lungful of pre-thunderstorm stickiness. This wasn't my night.

"Who's that?" Abbie asked, spotting a tall woman hovering around my car.

I squinted. "I have no idea."

The woman smiled as Abbie and I approached. "Is this your car?"

My eyes instantly scanned for signs of body damage. "Yeah."

"I wanted to make sure you saw this." She stepped aside, gesturing to the front tire. "You parked in glass. Your tire is flat."

What a lousy, lousy night. "Of course it is." I bent to examine it, as if I knew anything about cars.

Abbie shrugged. "Just put the spare on."

"Great idea." I pushed myself off the ground. "Do you know how to change a tire?"

Her eyes narrowed. "I would if I had a car."

"My son can change it for you," the woman offered. She had a relaxing quality to her, as if she constantly soothed everyone around her.

"That would be great," I said. "Thank you."

"No problem." She offered her hand. "I'm Amy, by the way."

"Skylar."

"Nice to meet you, Skylar." She turned to Abbie, then waved at someone beyond us. "Here he is."

I turned to see Amy's fabulous son who'd change my tire and get me on my way. Of course. I looked away from him, biting my lip to keep from screaming with frustration.

"Skylar, this is my eldest, Connor, and his brother, Chris. Boys, this is Skylar and—oh dear, I haven't asked your name yet."

Abbie smiled. "Abbie."

"Oh, I love the name Abbie." Amy clasped her hands together. "I wanted to name a girl Abigail Amelia, after my two sisters, but I ended up with a houseful of boys. My other two are in the car." Amy waved to the minivan parked several spots down. Out came a pair of auburn-headed boys. "That's Cameron, my second grader, and Curtis, who'll leave me this year to start kindergarten. Boys, this is Skylar and her sister, Abbie."

Curtis's forehead creased. "They don't look like sisters."

Amy gave him an adoring smile and smoothed his hair. "Not all brothers and sisters look as alike as the four of you. Now shake their hands and tell them how nice it is to meet them."

Cameron, an eight-year-old version of Connor, grinned as he stuck out his hand. "Nice to meet you," he said in a robust voice. I couldn't help smiling when I saw his missing front teeth.

A moment of silence followed, then Amy remembered why we'd met in the first place. "Oh, Connor, Skylar's tire has gone flat. Would you mind changing it?"

He caught my icy glare and shifted his weight. "Sure."

"See this front left one? She parked in glass."

Connor crouched beside the tire for a moment. "Where do you keep your jack?"

"I don't know."

"You have one, right?" he asked, brushing past me.

I followed him to the back of the car. "I don't know."

"Why would you drive without knowing if you have a jack?"

"Because I've never changed a tire."

He took my keys and popped the trunk. "What about someone like me who's changing your tire for you?"

"What are you looking for?" I asked as he stared into my empty trunk.

"Lots of drivers store handy items back here. A spare tire, a car jack, jumper cables."

"I don't even know what jumper cables are."

Connor flinched, as if my ignorance personally wounded him. "You should get married young."

A sharp remark waited on my tongue, but then, like magic, Connor pulled up the floor of my trunk.

I peered into the space Connor uncovered. "I didn't know that was there."

"Well, no jack, but at least you have an inflated spare." Connor tugged the tire from the car. "We can borrow my mom's jack, but you really need to get one of your own. And jumper cables. And learn how to use them."

"Or I could call AAA, who won't lecture me."

Connor smiled like I'd been joking, then strolled to the van, whistling. I stayed by the car, running my hand over the grooves of the spare tire, eavesdropping on Amy and Abbie. It was all small talk, what classes Abbie was in, her extracurriculars.

"Hey." Eli startled me. "I lost you in there. What's going on?"

I glanced from Eli to Connor, who had his back to us as he rummaged through the back of the minivan. "My tire's flat because I parked on glass—"

"Oh no. I bet Max or someone could change it for you."

Connor chose that moment to return, carrying a contraption I assumed was a jack, although it looked like too simple a tool to lift my car. "Hey, Eli."

"Connor's changing the tire for me." I tried to sound nonchalant, but the words came out too high.

"I didn't know you were still here," Connor said. "You're welcome to change her tire instead."

"Nah, that's fine." Eli's arm snuck around my waist. "I need to get home. Thanks for helping out my girl."

"Yeah, sure." Connor lifted the spare from the trunk. "Skylar, you'll want to come up front with me."

"Why?"

"Because I'm going to teach you how to do this." When I hesitated, he rolled his eyes. "Never mind. Just call AAA next time."

I offered Eli a strained smile. "I guess I'm going to learn how to change a tire."

"Great," he said with a squeeze of my waist. "Now if we're driving somewhere and get a flat, you can take care of it." He pulled me close and gave me a long good-bye kiss. "Call me when you get home."

It always frazzled me when Eli did this, but not in the way I wanted. When a guy like Eli kisses you, your body should react in some way—weak knees, a pounding heart, sweaty palms. I never had any of these.

But these concerns could wait.

I joined Connor and found Cameron already crouched beside him. "I'm learning how to change a tire too," he said, his chest puffed out.

For the next twenty minutes, Cameron and I observed Connor backing the car away from the glass, jacking it up, removing the tire, replacing it with the spare, and lowering the car.

Connor grunted as he tightened the final bolt. "It's easy, really. Once you've done it a couple times, you'll have it down."

"I don't intend to ever have to do this," I said.

He handed the jack to Cameron. "Put this back in the van for me, okay?"

"He's really cute," I said as Cameron scampered away.

My face warmed, as if I'd revealed some secret part of myself to Connor, but all he said was, "Most people say he looks just like me," and then gestured to my damaged tire. "Grab that side and we'll put this in the back. You should take it to your mechanic. They can probably patch it."

With the tire closed in the trunk, he stood there and looked at me. I knew I should say something. "I guess I'll see you at school tomorrow."

"I guess so."

"Thanks for changing my tire."

Connor shrugged. "It wasn't a big deal." His tone made it clear that he didn't like me any more than I liked him. Though standing near him, with the sunlight fading and his face sweaty from working on my car, I couldn't remember why we didn't get along. I evaluated him.

"You're a really nice guy."

This seemed to surprise Connor. "Thanks." He smiled.

And then it happened, that flurry of activity you get in your stomach when you like someone. Only I couldn't like Connor. He was short and goofy and, most important of all, Jodi's boyfriend.

I needed to get out of there.

Abbie and I thanked the Ross family again before climbing into the car.

"Amy's nice, isn't she?" Abbie said, flipping through radio stations.

"Uh-huh."

"They're all really nice."

I thought of Connor bent over my tire, forehead lined with concentration. "Yeah."

Just nice. I had to remember that.

4

"So, I'll just meet you at the car after school," I said to Abbie as we neared the sophomore hallway.

"I know the drill," she said, veering off.

I stood there for a moment, watching her walk away. "Have a great day," I said to myself.

"Skylar!" one of my friends called from behind me.

I groaned internally, then put on a smile and waved at Lisa and Alexis.

"Can you believe we're seniors?" Alexis said for at least the fifth time in the last twenty-four hours.

Lisa sniffled, and as they joined me, I noticed her puffy eyes. "I can't believe I'm starting my senior year without John. There should be, like, a law against breaking up with someone as the school year starts."

I fought off a jibe about them getting back together before Fall Ball. "Maybe it's better this way. You get to start senior year free and clear."

"I don't want to be free and clear." Lisa leaned her weight on me as we meandered down the senior hall. "I want to be with John."

I looked over her head to Alexis, hoping she'd say something encouraging. Instead, she pointed down the hall.

"That girl is wearing my shirt. I *just* bought it. Remember, Skylar? You were there."

"It was on the clearance rack," I said.

Alexis frowned. "So?"

"So, you can't buy something for four dollars and be surprised when every other girl is wearing one. They're priced to move."

She gave the shirt one last wistful look. "But still . . ."

"John bought this shirt for me. For my birthday last year." Lisa raised her tear-filled eyes. "Remember?"

Only because she reminded me every time she wore it.

"Liven up, okay?" I said as we approached our lockers. "You can't let John see you like this."

"What does it matter?" Lisa asked with a sigh, but she straightened up all the same.

We heard Jodi's laughter long before we turned the corner. We found Eli standing in front of our lockers, entertaining Jodi with a story. Her hand rested on his arm, and even though she had the courtesy to retract it when I arrived, I didn't like that he'd allowed it to be there.

"What's so funny?" Alexis asked. She couldn't stand being left out of anything.

"Oh, Eli was just telling me the most hilarious stories about youth group last night." Jodi looked at me. "It sounds so lame. How did you stand it?"

"Just the games," I said, surprised to feel protective. "Everything else was fun."

"What about circle time?" Eli tilted his head and said in an airy, Heather-like voice, "How can I be praying for you this week?"

Jodi laughed again. "I hate that."

"People caring about you?" I muttered.

"Adults pretending to be your friend," Jodi said, her voice cool. "What's with you today, Skylar?"

I focused on adjusting my locker shelf. "Nothing."

"You've been acting really weird for the last couple weeks," Jodi said. "I mean, since when are you defensive of church activities?"

"I said the games were lame. How is that being defensive?" I turned to face her and found Connor had joined our group. "Oh. Hi."

"Hi."

They all watched us, as if Connor and I carried on some fascinating conversation. I averted my eyes and hitched my messenger bag onto my shoulder. "You ready, Eli?"

"Sure." His arm slipped around me. "Anyone else have American History first hour?"

Everyone said no, and then Connor cleared his throat. "I do."

Again we looked at each other.

"I'll just meet you there," he said.

Jodi laughed and shook her head. "Don't stick around here just to worship and adore me," she said, batting her eyelashes. "My first class is on the other side of school, and I needed to leave like five minutes ago to make it on time."

Connor replied with a strained smile and then joined Eli and me on our short walk to American History.

"So Skylar says she's now an expert tire changer, thanks to you," Eli said, sounding oddly cheerful.

"Hmm," Connor said.

For some reason, this made Eli look at me and roll his eyes. I turned away.

Mr. Huntley taught American History. As a former seventh grade teacher, he often ran class like it was middle school, so it wasn't a surprise to find the desks arranged in groups of four rather than organized in rows. John already sat at a desk, and we joined him.

"Is Lisa in this class?" John's eyes darted between my face and the door, as if she might appear at any moment.

"No, you're safe."

He pushed his schedule across the table to me. "Tell me I don't have any classes with her."

I skimmed it. "Advanced Bio."

"You're sure?"

I nodded and returned the paper to him. "It's the only class she and I have together."

John groaned.

"What's the big deal?" Eli asked, seemingly irritated by his friend's dramatic flair. "It's just Lisa."

"Lisa said if she saw me today, she'd have to be restrained from clawing my eyes out."

"It's just talk. That's what girls do."

"Excuse me?" I said.

"Except for you, of course." Eli flashed a smile, the magic one that sometimes worked even on me. When I returned the smile, he pressed his fingertips into the back of my neck. "There's my girl. I wondered if I'd see you at all today."

"Was Lisa really mad?" John broke in.

"She was sad," I said. "I don't think she understood your timing."

John gnawed at a nonexistent nail. "It just wasn't working is all. We've tried, and we're not good as a couple."

"You can't help that, man." Eli stretched his arm around my shoulders. "And there's no good time to tell a girl that kind of stuff."

"Could I get a couple volunteers to pass out textbooks?" Mr. Huntley asked as the bell sounded. The hands of teacher's-pet hopefuls shot into the air. Mine remained flat on my desk.

After reading through the roster, Mr. Huntley dropped his glasses low on his nose and surveyed the room.

"I suppose you've all noticed the seats are arranged in a manner conducive to group work. You'll be working as teams quite a lot this year, and"—he looked around once more—"yes, this looks good. These will be your assigned seats."

Great. I glanced at Connor and caught him looking at me. He appeared just as thrilled to be stuck together.

After class—and after Eli pecked my cheek good-bye, as if it would be much longer than third period before we saw each other again—I nearly collided with Connor in the hall.

I weaved around him. "Great place to stand."

He followed me. "I think we should talk."

My heart raced. Last night, did he feel the same thing as me? That sharp burst of attraction? "What do we have to talk about?"

"There's a lot going on in your life right now, and—"

I stopped to face him, and he scrambled back a few steps. "That is *not* something we're going to discuss," I said. "Not ever. Especially not here. You got it?"

"Why do you assume I want to tell people what I overheard? It's none of my business. I wish I didn't even know."

"That makes two of us."

"But the fact is I *do* know, and none of your friends seem to."

"Do you have a point?"

Connor laughed, obviously amused. "I'm trying to tell you that if you want to talk I'm available, but I don't know why I'm offering, because it's obvious you don't want to talk to me." He turned and walked the opposite direction.

"Connor!" Did I just call after him?

He stopped and looked back. So now I needed to say something.

"Thanks." No reaction. "For the offer. It's nice."

The corners of his mouth twitched into a smile. "You're a surprising girl, Skylar Hoyt." He followed this with a salute, then fell into step with the crowd.

Most surprising of all—I meant what I said.

That night, as Mom passed me the moo shoo pork, she said, "I met someone you know at the women's brunch."

"Who would I know at the women's brunch?"

"Amy Ross, Cameron's mother. I told her thank you for assisting with your tire."

It took me a couple seconds to realize she meant Connor. "You mean *Connor's* mother."

"Oh, is Connor your age?" She looked at Abbie. "Cameron must be your age."

Abbie shook her head. "Chris."

Mom sighed, cutting into lemon chicken with her fork. “This is why parents shouldn’t do cute things like start their kids’ names with the same letter. It’s confusing. And surely it’s challenging for them as well. I’m forever mixing up your names, and they couldn’t be more different.”

“Do we have soy sauce, Teri?” Dad asked.

“In the pantry. The same place it always is.” While Mom’s words sounded pleasant enough, I caught her left eye twitching. I knew to look because mine did the same thing. One of Mom’s and my many similarities.

Abbie, who had yet to understand these little speeches of Mom’s didn’t require a response, said, “Amy’s sisters are named Abigail and Amelia, so she must like having a similar name to her sisters.”

“Hmm,” Mom said. “Well, they invited us over for dinner on Sunday, so don’t make any plans that evening.”

“All of us have to go?” I asked.

“Of course.”

I stabbed at a spear of broccoli. “Even me?”

Mom blinked at me. “What kind of a question is that? Of course you have to go.”

“Skylar and Connor don’t get along,” Abbie said.

Mom’s dark eyes accused me, as if she knew I was at fault. “Skylar, Connor Ross is a very nice young man. He fixed your tire, for heaven’s sake. There’s no reason you shouldn’t get along with him.”

This seemed strange, considering she’d never met him.

“We get along fine,” I said. “We’re just not friends.”

“Well, I don’t see why not.”

“Because she’s rude to him,” Abbie said.

I shot a deadly glare across the table.

"Oh, Skylar, we raised you better than this," Mom said.

"Actually, you raised me to not even look at boys, let alone be nice to them."

"Watch the attitude, Skylar," Dad said, one of the limited comments he ever made at the table. He didn't listen to content, just tones.

"You can be polite to someone without encouraging them," Mom said. "That's all I ask."

"Well, that's what I'm doing."

"Good. Then on Sunday we can have a perfectly lovely evening."

"What's happening on Sunday?" Dad asked.

Mom studied him for a moment, as if he might be joking. As if Dad ever joked. "We're going over to the Rosses'. That's what we've been discussing this entire time. Haven't you been listening?"

"Who are the Rosses?"

"A family at church. We're having dinner with them Sunday night. Really, Paul, you can't spend even twenty minutes at night paying attention to me and the girls?"

"I can't go," Dad said. "I'm working on Sunday."

"Sunday *night*?"

"No, but I'll have been in the office all day and won't feel like exchanging pleasantries with a family I've never met."

"You've worked every weekend this month. Take one lousy day off."

Dad's face burned red while Mom appeared serene. She and I were like ducks, I often thought, calm and collected above the surface, but chaotic underneath.

"I have responsibilities," Dad said tersely.

"You have responsibilities here as well. Maybe your daughters would like to see you every once in a while."

He glanced at us. "They have their own lives."

"Are you the only person working at that company? Because that's the only feasible explanation for why you're there so much."

Dad gritted his teeth. "I have responsibilities, Teri. One of which is paying off your credit cards."

"May I be excused?" I asked.

Eyes locked to Dad, Mom said, "You and Abbie are both excused."

Their grumblings reached us even as we jogged upstairs, but they faded into the background the way traffic does when you live on a busy street all your life. No surprise, Abbie locked her bedroom doors and cranked her stereo. I cringed at the sound of her pop music and called Eli.

"You're never going to believe what I just found out," I said, plucking at the lace of my duvet. "Guess where I'm having dinner this Sunday."

"The White House?"

"With the Rosses."

Silence. Then, "As in Connor Ross?"

"Yeah. His mom and my mom met at a brunch this morning, and now I have to eat dinner over there. Weird, huh?"

"Weird," Eli agreed. "And there's no getting out of it?"

"Mom seems pretty adamant that Connor and I are going to get along. Clearly she's never met him." More silence. "Eli?"

"You said your mom is crazy strict about guys, but she's encouraging this thing with Connor?"

I could hear the jealousy lining his words, tightening his voice, only I didn't know how to fix it. "I don't know why she's acting like this. I guess she just really likes Amy."

"Who?"

"Connor's mom."

"She doesn't like my mom?"

"She likes your mom."

"I don't see her forcing you on me."

"She's not forcing me on Connor. Her exact words regarding him were for me to be polite but not encouraging. Does that sound like forcing?"

"Is something going on between you and Connor?"

I forced a laugh. "Do you mean other than my intense dislike for him?"

"I saw you guys talking this morning after history."

"Yeah, we were arguing."

"What do you and Connor have to argue about?"

"I told you there's nothing going on. Why can't you just believe me?"

No answer.

I blew at my long bangs and waited a few seconds. "So, what, you're not talking to me now?"

Dead air.

I pulled my cell phone from my ear and found it flashing, "Call ended." He'd hung up on me? Did he think I was like every other girl he'd dated, who'd frantically redial his number, desperate to right the situation?

I powered off my phone. "Take that."

5

The banners announcing "Fall Ball is September 20th!" put Lisa in a funk the moment we got to school.

"This is going to be the first year I don't have a date. Couldn't he have held off a few more weeks?"

I sighed, sick of Lisa's whining. "We'll find you a date."

"Find me a date," Lisa repeated mockingly. "I'm one of *those* girls now, who's so pathetic her friends have to force some guy to go with her. Like last year when Eli went to prom with Jodi just because you already had a date. Everyone knew he only asked Jodi so he could hang around you." She sniffled. "I bet Eli's already asked you to Fall Ball, hasn't he? I bet he spent a lot of time thinking of the perfect way to do it."

"I'm his girlfriend, he doesn't need to ask me."

Lisa gave me a horrified look. "Yeah he does."

"Why? Isn't it understood?"

"It's understood that you'll say yes, but he should still ask. It's romantic."

"Eli's many things," I said, "but romantic is not one of them."

"Sure he is. He pursued you all these years—"

I interrupted with wry laughter. "And we got together at

a gas station after the worst night of—" I stopped myself. "Never mind. Eli's not going to ask. He's my boyfriend."

Lisa sighed. "I miss that, having an understood date."

"You want him?" I asked, fingers raking through my hair with frustration.

Lisa snapped out of her sorrowful state. "Is something wrong?"

I remembered Connor crouched beside my flat tire, the back of his neck damp with sweat. "Nothing. Just a little disagreement."

"A disagreement? What happened?" Lisa asked as we turned into the locker hall. Alexis and Jodi stood there conversing about the obvious fake bakers in our class, although they left themselves off the list.

"Hey, guys," Jodi said. She noticed my pink plastic sandals. "Great shoes. Very retro."

"They were my mom's like fifteen years ago. I found them in her closet."

"Enough about shoes," Lisa said. "We were talking about you and Eli."

"What about you and Eli?" Jodi asked. She appeared suspicious, as if I'd left her out of the loop.

"Nothing, I don't even remember what I was saying," I lied, coloring my lips with a deep berry gloss.

"Ooh, pretty." Alexis reached for it. "Can I have some?"

I passed her the tube.

"Why are things just 'fine' with you and Eli?" Lisa pressed.

"I thought things were great with you and Eli." Alexis paused to press her lips together. "You're a major PDA couple."

"Ick," I said, followed by a dramatic shudder. "Don't tell me that."

She puckered her mouth. "How does it look?"

"Your coloring is all wrong," I said.

"No fair." Alexis wiped her mouth with the back of her hand. "Tan people get to wear all the fun colors."

I gave her a look. "I'm not tan. I'm Hawaiian."

Eli appeared in the hallway, John in tow. John passed Lisa a nervous glance, but she feigned oblivion and turned to her locker.

"Morning, girls," Eli said. His eyes swept over my friends before landing on me. "You ready?"

I shrugged and threw my bag over my shoulder.

Jodi turned to Alexis and staged an aside comment. "Connor never lets me carry my own backpack. Isn't that so sweet?"

"I carry Skylar's," Eli said, his eyes narrowed. "I was just about to take it from her."

"I can carry my own bag," I said.

Eli turned on a smile that would charm even his sworn enemy. "This is a game she likes to play. She's so independent."

I ignored this and walked away, not caring if Eli followed. He did.

Eli attempted to take my bag. "Come on, Skylar."

"This isn't a competition. You don't have to carry mine just because Connor carries Jodi's."

"I'm your boyfriend. I should carry your backpack."

I picked up my pace. "Yeah, you also shouldn't hang up on me, but I don't see that stopping you."

"I didn't hang up on you. My phone died. I tried calling

you back for the rest of the night but all I got was voice mail." He jammed his hands into his pockets. As if he intended to say it under his breath, he added, "Now I *wish* I'd hung up on you."

I couldn't help laughing. "And you call John a drama queen."

"You said I'm a drama queen?" John piped in from behind us.

Eli paid no attention to him. "You know, all I wanted to hear you say last night was you have no feelings for Connor, and you never did."

"You're right, I didn't. I told you I have feelings of intense dislike for him. That's not enough for you?"

"I think you're lying."

"Well, I don't care."

"That's obvious." He pushed ahead of me into the classroom.

Connor already sat at our assigned table. Eli took his seat, and when I went for the desk beside him, he slapped his hand over the chair. "No way."

I snorted. "You've got to be kidding me."

"Not until you tell me what you two were arguing about yesterday."

"Why is that any of your business?" I asked, doing my best to disregard Connor's and John's curious stares.

"Because I'm your boyfriend."

I wrestled my chair from under his hand and plopped in it. "Well, you won't be for much longer if you don't stop acting like a baby." I glared at Eli as I scooted to the table. "Don't tell me where to sit ever again." Then I pulled my textbook from my bag and fake read.

John sat in the chair across from me as if taking a seat on an active volcano. Connor returned to his sketching, but Eli just sat there and watched me. I'd made it through an entire page before he said, "Please don't be mad at me." Beneath the table, his fingertips found my knee. "You're right, okay? It's none of my business, and I was being stupid and jealous. Just please don't be mad."

I made the mistake of looking at him. His expression, remorse with a hint of pain, bewitched me far more than his smile. I caused that. I, Skylar Hoyt, broke the great Eli Welling. I couldn't remember him ever apologizing to anyone. A strange sense of empowerment rushed through my body.

I placed my hand over his and squeezed. "I shouldn't have assumed you hung up."

He smiled and leaned to kiss me, declaring the fight over.

I stood at the sink brushing my hair into a ponytail when Abbie emerged from throwing up. She leaned against the doorway and looked at me through the mirror, her eyes dim with a strange look of defeat.

"I'm miserable," she said.

"Girls?" Mom called up the stairs. "It's time to go."

"Just a second!" I said.

"Where are we going?" Abbie asked, her voice hoarse.

"It's Sunday night." She shook her head, still unsure. "The Rosses."

She groaned. "Like that's what I need right now, to sit around with all their perfect kids." She exited through my room and walked to the edge of the stairs. "Mom? I don't feel good. I'm going to stay home."

"Abigail Marie Hoyt, you'll do no such thing!"

"You'd really expose the entire Ross family to my germs?"

"Fake germs aren't contagious, so I'm sure they'll be fine. Now, hurry up or we'll be late."

Abbie reentered my room. "Can you please get me out of going?"

"Please come." My tone sounded desperate as well. "I don't want to deal with Connor on my own."

"But I'm a wreck. I just spent the last ten minutes hugging the toilet, and"—she plucked at her shirt—"I should have thrown this thing out ages ago."

"Then brush your teeth and change your shirt."

"All my good clothes are dirty. How much longer do you think it'll be before Mom caves and does laundry?"

I hesitated a moment. "Do you want to borrow something of mine?"

Abbie gave me a wary look. "Is that a joke?"

I shook my head.

"I can borrow anything I want?"

"Sure."

Abbie peeked into my open closet doors. "Even your Juicy jeans?"

I cringed. "If you're really careful."

"I'll be careful." Abbie lifted them from their hanger like a precious artifact.

"I mean really, really careful. Like your-life-depends-on-not-ruining-these-jeans careful."

She plucked my lace-up sandals from the floor. "I love these."

"No, I'm wearing those." But Abbie had already grabbed the shoes and headed to her room. If I wasn't so relieved to be back on friendly terms, she never could've gotten away with disrupting a planned outfit.

Mom scowled when Abbie and I came downstairs. "We're going to be late." She ushered us through the garage door. "Already your father is irritated about tonight. The last thing I need is the two of you dragging your feet."

"Sorry, Mom," we chorused.

"Honestly, it feels like I'm the only one concerned with how our family appears," Mom continued as we walked to the idling car. Dad sat in the driver's seat, fingers tapping the steering wheel with impatience. "Being late to a social engagement, especially the first, is incredibly rude and inconsiderate."

At the Rosses', Mom made profuse apologies for our tardiness, even though it was barely five minutes past seven.

"Nonsense," Mr. Ross said, bubbling over with hospitality. "Come in, come in. Teri, Paul, I'm Brian. It's nice to meet you."

Dad put on his best smile, the one he used for clients. "Likewise, Brian." He offered his hand to him, then Amy. "Thanks for having us over."

"Were my directions okay?" Amy asked, wiping her hands on her apron. With the sprinkling of flour in her hair, she looked like an advertisement for the 1950s.

"Your directions were perfect," Dad said. "When you live with two princesses, getting out the door can take awhile."

Abbie turned red. I ground my teeth.

"Believe me, four boys aren't much easier." Amy winked at Abbie and me. "What a great dress, Skylar. And Abbie, I didn't remember your hair being so red. Brian, who does Abbie's hair remind you of?"

He studied my sister. "Martha."

"Exactly who I thought of. Martha is Brian's youngest sister." Amy reached for the fruit salad Mom held. "Thanks so much for bringing something, Teri."

"I was happy to," Mom said. I flinched at the sight of the supermarket packaging. Couldn't she at least have dumped it into a different bowl? Maybe one without the price stamped on it?

At the sound of a dog barking, Amy called, "Boys, will someone let him in?"

"Can I help you with anything, Amy?" Mom asked.

"Sure. Brian is doing most everything on the grill, but I'm getting the pies ready to go in the oven."

"I don't know if I'd allow Teri in the kitchen." Dad's voice teemed with testosterone. "Those pies might burn if she so much as glances at the oven."

Brian smiled politely and Amy chirped a good-natured, "Nonsense!"

With that, the adults left Abbie and me in the entryway to find our own entertainment. Seconds later, a Westland Terrier burst into the room, Cameron at his heels. "Don't pet him! Don't pet him!"

Abbie froze, her hand halfway to the tiny dog. "Why not?"

Cameron leaned against the wall, panting. "He'll pee on you. Let him calm down." He turned his golden-green eyes up at me and grinned. One shoelace was untied, and his forehead sported a red sticker. When I smiled back at him, he ran from the entryway squealing.

Connor appeared from upstairs. "You'll have to excuse him. He has a crush on you."

"On me?" I said.

Cameron, who'd apparently been listening, cried out in anguish. "Connor!"

"Connor, don't embarrass your brother," Amy said from the kitchen.

Abbie cast a sympathetic look at the dog wiggling and whining at her feet. "Can I pet him now?"

Connor evaluated him. "I'd give it another minute or two."

"If that dog pees on my jeans, you're dead," I said so only Abbie could hear. Having his filthy paws all over them was bad enough.

"Come on in," Connor said, walking deeper into the house.

Growing up with a mom who regularly adjusted the color scheme of our home according to the latest design magazines, I'd developed the habit of judging people based on their decor. You could learn a surprising amount—like Lisa's family had money but no imagination. The rooms in their house always looked like catalog pages from Z Gallerie. Eli's mom grew up on a farm outside of Abilene, Kansas—*Country Living* could've featured their house.

With the Rosses', I expected one of two extremes—either one of those too-organized, over-labeled houses where you fear being shot for not using a coaster, or someplace ragged and worn down because they'd rather give the money to charity than buy themselves a new couch. Instead, I walked into their living room and thought, *Comfortable. Warm. Home.*

Rich-colored walls showcased family photos and the boys' artwork. Furniture filled the room—worn leather couches, corduroy chairs, and a coffee table that invited you to throw your feet up. Most surprising was the TV, larger even than ours. I'd assumed the Rosses spent evenings reading Bible stories rather than watching prime time.

Curtis sat cross-legged before the giant screen, too absorbed in his cartoon to acknowledge us. Cameron giggled when we entered and curled into a ball against the arm of a couch.

"Where's Chris?" Abbie asked, settling into an armchair.

Connor took a seat on the other couch. "I don't know."

Cameron's voice came muffled from behind a throw pillow. "He's upstairs getting ready."

"Ready for what?" Connor asked.

Cameron shrugged. He peeked at me over the pillow, giggled, and then hid himself again.

"Curtis, turn the TV down, buddy," Brian said as he carried a platter of barbecued chicken through the living room. The smell of not-lasagna made my mouth water.

"Can I pet your dog yet?" Abbie asked.

Cameron lowered the pillow from his face. "Yeah, you're safe."

She scratched behind his ears. "What's his name?"

"Kevin," Cameron answered. "But with a C so he doesn't feel left out."

I smiled. Should an eight-year-old make me smile more in five minutes than my boyfriend had all week?

Chris emerged from upstairs with a casual, "Hey." He sat beside Cameron and turned his eyes to the television, feigning indifference to our presence. The intense cologne smell he brought with him testified otherwise, as did his frequent glances at my sister.

Amy called us into the dining room. With cloth napkins and an abundance of food, this seemed more like Thanksgiving than August 24.

Cameron grinned as he handed me the basket of homemade rolls. "Do you like bread?"

"Yep."

He beamed up at me. "Me too," he said, as if this made us soul mates.

I ignored this and passed the rolls.

"Do you have a boyfriend?" he asked.

Everyone but me found this hilarious, even Mom, who became irritated when strangers suggested I was popular with boys.

"Focus on your food, Cam," Brian said. "There'll be plenty of time after dinner for flirting with Skylar."

Mom laughed and chose a piece of chicken for herself. "Sorry, Cameron, but Skylar isn't allowed to date until college."

I couldn't keep from glancing at Connor, who looked back at me with surprise.

"Why not?" Cameron asked.

"It's the rules," Mom said.

Okay, time for a new subject. "Everything looks wonderful, Amy and Brian," I said as I heaped mashed potatoes onto my plate. When had I last eaten non-instant mashed potatoes?

"Skylar." Mom used her voice reserved for rebuking. "It's *Mister* and *Missus* Ross."

"Oh, please call us Brian and Amy," Brian said.

Mom shook her head. "She knows better."

"But we prefer it," Amy insisted. "To me, Mrs. Ross is my mother-in-law."

"Kids don't respect adults the way they used to," Dad said. He launched into an anecdote conveying how he never would have thought to call an adult by their first name when he was a kid.

But despite my disrespect of calling Amy and Brian what they preferred, the evening went well. So well, in fact, that during dessert my mother felt compelled to initiate a carpool.

"We live practically around the corner from each other. It doesn't make sense for both you and Skylar to drive all the way to the high school," Mom said. "Skylar will happily take Connor and Chris."

Amy stirred cream into her coffee as she contemplated this. "We plan to get Connor a car soon. They could trade off weeks or something. If it's okay with Skylar, it'd be a great help."

"Of course it's okay with Skylar." Mom turned to me, eyes commanding me to agree.

"Sure." I forced up the corners of my mouth. "It's no problem."

How did this happen? Six weeks ago, Connor was just an annoying guy who my best friend liked. Now our dads had a standing golf date, our moms were swapping recipes (as if mine cooked), and I'd be hauling him and his little brother to and from school.

And of course, we got stuck together after dessert. Cameron and Curtis splashed about the pool, and Chris and Abbie occupied the swing set. Their conversation appeared intimate, leaving me with no option but to join Connor on the back porch swing.

"So, you're not allowed to date until college," Connor said as I sat.

I groaned. I should have interrupted Chris and Abbie. "Something like that."

"That's interesting. Since you have a boyfriend."

"Do you have a point?"

"No, no point." He pushed his feet against the ground, lulling the swing into motion. "It just seems strange that—"

"Are you incapable of having a nice, normal conversation?" I said. "Whatever happened to questions like, how'd you do on the bio test, or, where are you thinking of going to college?"

Connor grinned. "Where are you thinking of going to college?"

I gave him a look. "You really want to know?"

"I'm in a hospitable kind of mood."

"Great," I said with a laugh.

A long silence ensued as I watched Cameron and Curtis compete for the best belly flop.

"So, are you going to answer the question?" Connor asked.

"Oh, sorry. I think I'll just go to Johnson County Community. I don't know what I want to do, so . . ."

"Yeah, same here." Connor folded his arms behind his head. "I'd like to stay at home awhile longer."

I relaxed against the swing. "That might be the only reason I apply somewhere else."

He followed my gaze to Abbie. "How's everything going with . . . that?"

"I thought we agreed you'd never bring it up," I said in a frosty voice.

"Right." But he seemed completely unintimidated by my ice princess act. "So. Is Eli the first guy you've dated?"

I rolled my eyes. "Connor."

"You dated a guy named Connor?"

"No, I meant I don't want to talk about this anymore."

"So you *didn't* date a guy named Connor."

"No."

"Am I the only Connor in your life?"

"There isn't room for another Connor. You're more Connor than I can handle."

He laughed. "You know, you're really funny. You should be this way when we're with other people."

"Funny?"

"No," Connor said. "Yourself."

I looked at him. "What do you mean?"

"When we're with other people, you're so . . ."

"I'm so what?" I attempted to sound forceful enough to make Connor rethink this whole line of conversation.

"Cliché," he said.

"Cliché!" Far worse than the profane description I assumed he'd assign me. "I'm *anything* but a cliché."

His eyes widened. "I didn't know you'd take it so personally."

"I've never been told something so offensive in my entire life." I could feel the twitch of my left eye as I struggled to hold in tears. "What makes me a cliché?"

"Maybe that's not the right word," Connor said, fidgeting. "You just come across like the typical rich, popular girl."

"That's not true." I heard Aaron's voice in my head, saying I was different than my friends. "My friends, they're the ones who are typical popular girls."

"I'm not saying you *are* a typical popular girl. Just that you pretend to fit in. But not all the time. Only when we're at school. Or church. Or around our families." He set the swing into motion again. "But now, when it's just us, you're different. You're being yourself. Not putting on a show."

"Putting on a show?" How could he possibly think such horrible things when everything about me screamed "unique"? Would someone desperate to fit in wear clothes like I did? My stupid friends would certainly never attempt my outfits. They wore nothing without Gap's stamp of approval.

My tears broke through. "I can't believe that's what you think of me."

"Are you crying?" Connor looked at me with wide eyes. "I'm so sorry. We can go back to me bugging you about Eli and you telling me to shut up. I didn't mean to hurt your feelings."

"You know, I thought we were going to be friends." I didn't realize this until the words spilled from my mouth.

Connor appeared panicked. "We are."

"Leave me alone," I said as I stood.

He gripped my arm, holding me there beside him. "Skylar, please. I want us to be friends too. Please forgive me."

I looked at him, into his eyes. He looked sincere. "Regardless of what you think, I'm not putting on a show or trying to fit in. I mean, look at me."

He did. I squirmed. "Should clothes be what make you unique?"

"It's *not* just my clothes."

"Please, just forget about it. All I was trying to say is I'm having fun with you tonight."

Connor's expression, soft and hopeful, convinced me to reclaim my seat. I sucked in a wobbly breath, hoping to dissipate the tears still pooling behind my eyes. "I think we should strive to have one of those relationships where we don't really talk to each other. It seems safer."

"Okay," he said, and we swung in silence as the sunlight faded.

A soft knock sounded on the door between my room and the bathroom. Then it slid open and Abbie peeked through the crack. "Skylar?" She'd been crying.

I sat up. "What's wrong?"

"Can I get in bed with you?"

"Sure." I scooted against the wall. She settled beside me, careful not to touch.

After a minute's silence, she said, "I don't know what to do. Somehow I have to tell Mom and Dad."

I searched for the right words but came up with nothing. "Yeah . . ."

"They're going to kill me, right? I mean, there's no chance of them, like, driving to Babies R Us and buying up the store. They'll kick me out."

I didn't answer.

"This sucks." Abbie pounded her fist into my mattress. "*This* is why you're not supposed to have sex. And you want to know what else sucks? For the first time, I've actually met a really sweet, cute, Christian guy, and he's not even interested in me."

"What are you talking about?" I said. "Couldn't you smell Chris when he came downstairs? He's crazy about you."

Her voice emerged tight as she spoke through tears. "Only because he doesn't know me yet."

I smoothed her hair, like I'd seen mothers do on TV when they consoled their daughters, but it made Abbie cry harder.

As Abbie dozed off, I thought about Mom and Dad, ignorant across the hall. They deserved to know their fifteen-year-old daughter was pregnant. How much longer should I wait for Abbie to tell them? Would spilling Abbie's secret make me a responsible sister or a lousy one?

I fell asleep with these questions unanswered.

6

"I don't see what the big deal is," Mom said, watching from the kitchen table as I toasted a Pop-Tart. "Their house is on your way. It hardly adds any time to your drive."

I stared at my reflection in the toaster. "Maybe it's about more than time."

"I don't understand. You and Connor seemed to get along so well last night."

Just the sound of his name made my mouth go dry, my shoulders tighten. "We don't get along at all." But I could hear it in my voice. I liked him. How could I like him when I didn't *want* to like him? Shouldn't a person have some kind of control over that?

Abbie drained the last of her orange juice. "You ready?"

I forced the toaster to relinquish my Pop-Tart and we left.

At the Rosses', I'd barely pulled into the driveway when Cameron burst out the door in his pajamas. He frolicked barefoot to my side of the car.

"Look!" he cried as my window slid down. He opened his mouth and wiggled a bottom tooth.

I tried not to cringe. Even as a kid, loose teeth grossed me out. "Wow."

"I noticed it last night when I brushed my teeth. I worked on it 'til I fell asleep."

Crumbs of some kind dusted his hair. "Cameron, why are there crumbs in your hair?"

He shrugged as I brushed them away.

"Hey."

I jumped at the sound of Connor's voice. "You scared me."

He laughed. "By saying 'hey'? You need to get out more." Through the window, he handed me a paper plate with two warm, oversized muffins. "From Mom. She says as long as you're taking us to school, she'll provide breakfast for you guys."

"Wow, that's so nice," Abbie said, taking the muffins from me.

Amy stood in the doorway in sweatpants and sleepy eyes. She waved. "Thank you!"

I waved back. "Thank *you*!"

Why did Amy seem to care more about our day than our own mom, who'd lounged at the kitchen table while we scrounged up our own breakfast, and then didn't even say good-bye?

"Your mom is really great," I said to Connor at school after we'd split off from Abbie and Chris. "Have a bite of this muffin."

He smiled and shook his head. "No thanks, I already had two."

"You're so lucky." I popped the bite in my mouth. "I'd be so fat if I lived at your house. Do you guys eat like this all the time?"

"What do you mean?"

"What do you think I mean? Real mashed potatoes, homemade muffins."

"You're crazy," Connor said.

"And you're spoiled."

Instead of responding, Connor changed the subject. "You know, I think it would surprise people to know how good you are with kids."

I looked at him. Was he teasing? "I stink with kids."

"You're great with Cameron and Curtis."

"I have no idea how to talk to anyone under age ten. You never know what they're going to say. That freaks me out."

"I wouldn't have guessed from how you are with my brothers."

A compliment from him, which normally I wouldn't notice, now made my head fuzzy, as if I'd chugged a bottle of NyQuil. I stole a peek at him. He hadn't cut his hair in a while, causing dormant curls to reveal themselves at his temples. All last week I'd found this maddening. I'd grabbed the scissors from my pencil bag and joked with Alexis about taking matters into my own hands. Now the curls seemed endearing. What was wrong with me?

We rounded the corner into the senior hall to find Eli and Jodi deeply involved in conversation. Eli leaned against the wall, arms crossed to flatter his biceps. Jodi twirled the ends of her hair onto a finger, her signature flirting move. When they spotted us, Eli straightened and Jodi's hands fell to her sides. They said in unison, "Hey."

Eli kissed me. "How was dinner?"

I shrugged as Connor said, "You should have seen Skylar with my brothers. They loved her."

"Skylar?" Jodi said. "She's horrible with kids."

Triumphant, I turned to Connor. "Told you so."

"Last Halloween," Jodi added, "when she was giving out candy, she made a little girl cry."

"This is true," I said.

Connor wagged his head. "How is that possible? They ring the doorbell, you give them candy, and they leave."

Jodi noticed the remainder of my muffin. "That looks good. Are they selling those in the cafeteria?"

"Amy gave it to me."

"Amy?"

"Connor's mom."

"Because Skylar took us all to school," Connor said.

"How come?" Eli asked. He kept running his fingers through my hair, reminding me why I rarely wore it loose around him.

"Oh, something our moms arranged." I waved my hand to show its insignificance.

"So, over the weekend my parents and I started discussing plans for my birthday party," Jodi said, twirling her hair again. "It's gonna be great. We'll have a catered dinner at my parents' house, and then they're going to rent a suite for us at the Raphael, and then—"

"What's this for?" Alexis asked as she joined us. "Your birthday?"

Jodi nodded. "Doesn't it sound perfect?"

"The perfectest."

"That's not a word," Connor said.

Alexis giggled and turned a toothy smile on him. "It is so a word." Did she have to be so flirty all the time?

"No it's not."

"Well, it should be."

"There's no need to improve the word 'perfect.' It doesn't get any better than perfect."

"Like Skylar," Eli said.

I blinked at him. "What?"

"No need for improvement." He smiled, proud of the compliment.

I forced myself to smile back. "I need to get to class early. I'll see you there."

"Nah, I'll come with you." He nodded at Jodi. "See you in Spanish."

As if Jodi merited her own special good-bye.

We started down the hall, and I searched his face for clues about what I'd just witnessed. Feeling my gaze, he turned to me. "You okay?"

"Oh yeah," I said in a bright voice.

His smile took on a tender nature. "She got moved into my Spanish class. That's why I said it."

"What are you talking about?" I asked.

"Oh, I thought you were wondering why I said good-bye to Jodi."

"Did you?" I shrugged. "I didn't notice."

He tucked an arm around my waist. "That's because you're the best girlfriend ever."

But the best girlfriend ever probably wouldn't smile at her boyfriend while glancing beyond him to spy on a friend of his. Who happened to have his arm around my best friend.

7

The bathroom pocket door was open, granting me a view of Abbie sprawled across her bed. She'd been lethargic all week, but still it surprised me that she appeared to have no plans on a Friday night. Even our parents had plans. Dinner with a client of my dad's, but still.

I thought she was asleep until I looked at her a second time while waiting for my curl to set. Her eyes were open.

"Where are you going tonight?" she asked.

I told her the same thing I'd told Mom. "Slumber party at Alexis's."

Her eyes noted my black mini and sequined shoes. "Girls night, huh?"

"Something like that." I released the lever of the iron. A steaming curl fell to my shoulder. "What are you doing tonight?"

"This."

"Why don't you go over to Jenna's?"

"Why don't you mind your own business?"

I didn't respond, and she didn't say anything else until I left the bathroom.

"Tell Eli I said hi," she said softly.

So on top of feeling guilty for lying to my mother, I now felt bad about Abbie.

"It's not that I owe her an explanation or anything, but recently I feel bad about our relationship," I said as I stirred my ravioli. "Like maybe I'm the reason we're not very close."

Eli answered with a shrug. "Do you need to be close?"

"It'd be nice. She's my sister."

"I'm not close to either of my sisters."

"That's different. You're a guy."

He raised a mischievous eyebrow at me. "How nice of you to finally notice."

The hairs on the back of my neck rose, as if I were a cat going on the defensive. "What does that mean?"

"Nothing."

"Seriously, what did you mean?"

He wagged his head at me. "Skylar, it was a joke. Lighten up."

I watched him return to his manicotti, cutting and chewing as normal. He really had been joking. I returned to my dinner as well. "Sorry. I guess I'm just bummed about this Abbie thing."

"I'll tell you what you need." Eli pointed his fork at me. "A good party. You know James on the baseball team? He's throwing one tonight. I thought we'd go after dinner, if it hasn't already been broken up."

"But I thought . . ." I changed my mind. "I don't know that I'm up for a party."

Eli looked at me as if I said I planned to shave my head. "What?"

I squirmed in my chair. "I thought it was just going to be the two of us tonight."

"So, you don't want to go?"

"Not really."

That mix of confusion and disgust remained on his face, so I averted my eyes.

"Is this about Aaron?" he asked.

I didn't answer, just kept pushing a square of ravioli through the cream sauce. Eli placed his hand over mine. "Skylar, that's not going to happen again."

"I can make sure of it if I don't go to any more parties," I said into my bowl.

"That's letting him win."

"What if he's there tonight?"

"He won't be. Aaron is in Florida at college."

"But what if he's in town for something?"

"If for some reason he's there, I promise you we'll leave."

"But I said no more parties."

I said it so quietly Eli asked me to repeat myself. When I did, he asked, "When did you say that?"

"The morning after."

"But it's not like you meant it," Eli said. "You weren't thinking clearly."

I remember him leaning in to kiss me as the gas tank clicked closer to full. Half my brain told me it was a bad idea, that it would create changes I didn't want. The other half wanted to be close to him, wanted to feel safe and secure. Eli was right, I hadn't been thinking clearly that morning.

I smoothed the tablecloth with my hands. "I was serious about no parties."

"I don't remember you saying no parties. I thought you said you were going to quit drinking. What's the harm in a party if you don't drink?"

The waiter interrupted to ask if he could get a box for me.

"Please," I said, pushing my plate at him.

"And bring the check, will ya?" Eli asked through a mouthful of mozzarella and red sauce. Charming.

"I thought we were going to do it together," I said when the waiter left.

He swallowed his enormous bite. "Do what?"

"The life change stuff. Church and all that."

He appeared puzzled. "I've been going to church."

"I know." I took a deep breath. Why couldn't I make him understand? "But I thought we agreed to no more parties."

Eli laughed. "So we can't have fun?"

"You need to be around a bunch of other drunk people to have fun with me?"

He sighed. "How's skipping the party going to make you a better person? Wasn't that the point of making changes to your life?"

"Well . . . yeah."

"Do you think going home and sitting alone in your room will make you a better person?"

"No . . ."

"Okay, then. What's the problem?"

"The problem is . . ." But now I felt incredibly lame. "I guess there isn't one."

Eli smiled, triumphant. "Good. Then we can go."

All the praying I did on the drive to the party, requesting that the cops had already broken it up, proved fruitless. Instead, the party was at the stage I used to love, deep enough into the night that everyone was buzzed and goofy, but still too early for vomiting and tearful breakdowns.

When I opened the door of James's house, the door that led into my old life, I spotted my group right away. Jodi was perched on the arm of the living room sofa, a burning cigarette in one hand and a plastic cup in the other. My friends crowded around her, as if she were the queen.

"There you guys are!" Jodi interrupted her own story. "I wondered if you were coming."

"You know Skylar," Eli said with a tweak of my ear. "Got to make an entrance."

Everyone laughed, which helped him to ignore my stony glare.

"I'll get us something to drink," he said before vanishing into the crowd.

"Here, Skylar." Jodi scooted to make room for me on the arm.

"No, I'm fine. I'll just sit—" I turned and found Connor occupying one of the armchairs. What was he doing here? "On the floor," I finished, dropping to a patch of the rug near the coffee table.

Jodi continued with her story, some tale from the wild world of working in retail, but I couldn't focus. Instead, my eyes drifted around the room, searching the faces. I knew Eli was right, that Aaron started at FSU this fall and had no reason to be at a high school party rather than Tallahassee. But that didn't slow the rapid thumping of my heart.

Eli settled beside me. "Here."

I looked into the plastic cup of beer and made a face at him.

"It's all they have," he said.

"Really? There's no running water in this house?"

"If you don't want it, don't drink it," Eli snapped, and then turned away from me.

I set my beer on the coffee table and ignored it. If only I could have wound the clock back a few hours and *met* Eli at the restaurant, then I could have gone home now. I'd been so excited about Mom and Dad being out of the house so Eli could pick me up like a real date. How long would I have to be here at this stupid party?

An hour later, when the mood shifted from buzzed and happy to drunk and stupid, I continued to ask myself that question. None of my friends showed any signs of weariness. They seemed not to notice repeated stories or too-loud laughing, and when Madison Embry caught her boyfriend kissing another girl, my friends cackled their way through her hysterical crying and dramatic exit.

"Serves her right." Jodi snickered. "Alexis, 'member when she did that to you with Seth and I punched her?"

Alexis laughed as if Jodi was doing a stand-up routine.

I bit my tongue to keep irritated words locked in my mouth and turned away.

That's when I saw him.

He started up the spiral staircase, his back to me, his arm around some dark-haired girl I didn't recognize. She leaned against him as if walking upstairs required too much effort. Had I done the same thing?

I leaped to my feet. The girl's head fell back with laughter, and I wanted to shake her, prevent her from falling into the horrible nightmare I'd been living.

But as I neared the base of the stairs, determined to call out Aaron in front of everybody, the couple turned and I saw my mistake. He didn't look a thing like Aaron. It was a trick played on me by the dim lighting mixed with paranoia.

I couldn't just stand there looking like an idiot, and I didn't want to answer any questions my friends might pose, so I escaped through the back door. Others were outside enjoying the warm August night. They lounged in or around the pool, leaving me sheltered on the side porch. I sat on the concrete slab as modestly as my miniskirt would allow, struggling not to cry.

When would this go away, this constant fear of Aaron, of what happened that night? Would I eventually go back to being myself? That's what I really wanted. To forget about Aaron, return to the party, and have the carefree fun I'd once had. I wanted to drink my beer, laugh, and not feel bad for Madison. It sure beat sitting here, looking at the vegetable garden James's mother planted that had little spikes coming out of the ground to mark zucchini and carrots. Reading those signs filled me with guilt. She was enjoying a vacation with her husband, clueless of my friends smoking in her house and spilling beer on her couch.

The door opened behind me.

"I'm sorry," I said, knowing I'd worried Eli when I fled without explanation. "I just couldn't sit there any longer."

"Believe me, I understand." It wasn't Eli, but Connor.

I turned. "Oh, hi."

He smiled and pushed his hands into his pockets. "Did you think I was Eli?"

I nodded.

"He's too busy flirting with my girlfriend to worry about his."

I sighed. "That should bother me, right?"

Connor crouched beside me. "Maybe you're just not surprised."

I didn't answer.

"Well, I've had all the partying I can stand. I'm taking off. You wanna come?"

I held his gaze for a moment. "Seriously?"

"Would it be nice to joke about that?"

"Not at all."

"Then it's a good thing I'm not." His knees cracked as he stood. "My mom just called. Cameron's at a birthday party and was supposed to spend the night, but I guess he got a little freaked out and wants Mom to come get him. I have her car, and Dad's out bowling with Chris and Curtis."

"So, we're picking up your brother in the minivan?"

Connor nodded. "Or you can sit around here and pretend you're drinking your beer and having a good time."

An excellent point.

"Let's go," I said, and accepted the hand he offered to help me stand. "I just have to tell Eli good-bye."

But when I saw him seated beside Jodi, his face red from laughing and his eyes crinkled with that smile, it didn't seem important for him to know I was leaving.

"Forget it," I muttered to Connor and pushed through the crowd.

As the door closed behind us, we heard the shattering of the first valuable of the night, a vase from the sound of it.

"I think we're getting out of here just in time," Connor said as we trekked across the grass toward his car.

"Just in time would imply we'd never come at all." I offered a wry smile. "I hate these stupid parties."

"That seems out of character."

"Well, it seems out of character for you to be here, so I guess we're even. I assume you're in the same boat I am? Jodi dragged you here?"

"Not exactly. James said it would be low-key." He held open the passenger door of Amy's minivan. "Does that mean Eli dragged you?"

"Something like that."

"You always struck me as a girl who'd enjoy a good party."

I hesitated. "Not anymore."

Connor looked at me, wordless. What did he see? And why did I care?

On the road, Connor and I said nothing to each other after he established I was free to adjust the air vents however I liked. I looked forward to Cameron joining us to break the stiff silence, but the little boy who climbed into the van differed from the kid I'd had dinner with last Sunday night.

I greeted Cameron with a warm smile. "Hey."

He scowled at me and buckled his seat belt.

"Not in much of a party mood?" I asked, craning my neck into an awkward position so I could see him from the front seat.

"No," he said.

"Yeah, me neither."

Then Connor got into the car, and I relinquished the responsibilities of cheering his brother up.

Except Connor didn't say anything.

I don't know why I felt obligated, I just did. I recognized the expression on Cameron's face, when something you anticipated didn't turn out like you thought. When you held yourself responsible for it.

As Connor turned onto my street, I cleared my throat. "You know, Cameron, your brother and I were at a party tonight too."

Cameron glowered at me. "I know. That's why my mom couldn't come get me."

"We were glad to leave." I turned to face him. "You know why?"

He looked like he didn't want to be curious but couldn't help it. "Why?"

"Because sometimes parties just stink."

"Yeah?" His smile was small, but it was there.

"Yeah. I'm so glad to be home," I said as the minivan rolled up my driveway.

Now Cameron gave me the full grin, missing teeth and all.

I popped open the door. "Thanks for the ride."

"No problem," Connor said. "And—" He nodded to the backseat, then mouthed "thank you."

Later, as I crawled into bed, it occurred to me that the night hadn't ended up too bad.

8

When I said hi to Lisa in biology on Monday, she looked at me with eyes of ice and then turned away.

"Okay." I took my seat. "I'm going to venture a guess that you're mad at me."

"Wow. You're, like, a genius, aren't you?" Her voice matched her eyes.

I sighed and pulled out my biology notes from the previous week. "Are you at least going to give me a clue about what I did?"

Lisa gave me a wary look, as if determining my sincerity. "I guess I shouldn't be surprised you're siding with her." She fluffed her hair. "It obviously didn't faze you to steal Eli from Jodi."

"Steal Eli from Jodi?" I struggled to keep my voice quiet. "They broke up freshman year. And I never pursued Eli. Not to mention that—" I shook my head. "But none of that's important. Who did I supposedly side with?"

"Alexis."

"Over what?"

Lisa's expression showed exasperation. "John."

"What about him?"

"Alexis and John are dating!"

Realizing she'd spoken much louder than intended, Lisa glanced around the room, her face red. A few students heard and laughed, but most were preoccupied with their own activities.

"When did that happen?" I asked.

She narrowed her eyes. "Don't play that game."

"Lisa, I seriously didn't know."

"How could you not know? Everybody who was at James's party saw them."

"I must have already left."

"When did you leave?"

"Around 10:30."

She chewed on her lip for a moment, considering this. "You really didn't know?"

"Of course not. How long has this been going on?"

"Since the end of the summer," Lisa said, her eyes filling with tears. "I guess it's why he broke up with me. Because of *her*."

"That doesn't make any sense," I said. "Wouldn't we all have noticed?"

"They're both just such good liars." She spit out "liars" like it tasted foul.

"Maybe this is good," I said, attempting to soothe. "Now you can finally get over him."

"Yeah, you're right. Who needs either of them?"

But a minute later when John entered the room and took a seat on the other side, she sagged against me, deflated.

It turned out to be a bad relationship day.

When I arrived at lunch, I found only Eli and John seated at our table. John foolishly met my gaze as I approached, and I fixed him with a withering glare. He sunk lower in his seat. What did Lisa and Alexis even see in him?

"Where's everyone else?" I asked.

"Where else do you girls go for big drama?" Eli said. "Bathroom."

I gave John a pointed look. "You are so not worth this."

I thought for sure I would walk into the bathroom and find Lisa and Alexis at each other's throats, but instead, I heard Jodi.

". . . like I'd be devastated. Can you believe that?" Her gaze snapped to me as I entered. "Nice of you to join us."

"Sorry," I said, although I wasn't sure why. "What's going on?"

"Like you don't know."

"I don't."

"Whatever." She pitched a balled-up paper towel into the trash can. "You're a horrible actress."

I looked to the other girls. "What's going on?"

No one answered at first. Finally, Lisa cleared her throat. "Jodi and Connor broke up."

"Oh, go ahead and say it." Jodi yanked a new paper towel from the dispenser. "He dumped me."

"Connor dumped you?" I asked.

"What an idiot, right? Does he think he can do better? If it weren't for me, he couldn't even hang out with us." She pointed a threatening finger at me. "You better not let him."

"When did this happen?"

"Like five minutes ago. He sat me down, acting like it was this big deal, like it was somehow going to hurt me to be dumped by him." She laughed, but it sounded hollow. "Connor. The guy who considers his black Adidas pants dressy."

Neither of the other girls seemed interested in speaking.

"You like him, though, don't you?" I said, my voice gentle. "It's okay to feel hurt."

"Skylar, it's Con-nor." Jodi emphasized each syllable. "I'm not hurt, I'm humiliated he beat me to it. I should've dumped him last week. Or before school started. Or I should've listened to you and never even given him a chance."

"Jo, calm down."

"I don't want to calm down!" She turned away from us and crossed her arms.

The girls gave me desperate looks. "Would you give us a few minutes alone?" I asked.

They filed out of the restroom. When the door swung shut, I rested a hand on Jodi's shoulder.

"I thought I would be the one to call it quits." Tears choked her words. "I thought he liked me more than I liked him. It was what I liked best, how safe he seemed. I thought he was incapable of hurting me."

I squeezed her hand. "I'm so sorry."

Bitterness eclipsed her sadness. "It's because of you, you know."

"What's because of me?"

"It's my own fault." She looked away from the wall, into my eyes. "I should always assume that guys prefer you."

"What? Connor doesn't prefer me."

She released a disbelieving laugh. "So it's a coincidence that he broke up with me just as you guys became friends?"

"We're not friends. Our parents are friends. That's it."

"You know, this is exactly what happened with Eli. He was perfectly content with me until you guys saw that movie together."

"Jodi, Connor is a completely different situation," I said. "And Eli and I were already at the theater when you called and said you couldn't make it."

"It was barely a week later when he broke up with me. He said he needed to focus on school, but of course I knew the truth." She gave the mirror a knowing smile. "I guess some things never change."

"Jodi," I started, but didn't know what to say.

She took a deep breath. "It was a nice idea, you coming in here, but maybe you should go."

"No, I—"

"Please go."

It seemed wrong to leave, but what choice did she give me? "I want to help."

"You can help by *not* dating him, okay?" Then she pushed past me and out the door.

"You're quiet," Connor said on our drive home. He'd been watching me ever since we got in the car, but Abbie and Chris had been silent until now, so this was our first semi-private moment.

"That's because I don't have anything to say."

"You and Eli still fighting?"

"Who says we're fighting?"

"I just assumed. I mean, you left James's party without saying good-bye. Didn't he think—"

"I don't know what Eli thought because we haven't talked about it, okay?" I hadn't realized how this angered me until I said it out loud. Eli hadn't said a word to me about the party. He hadn't asked how I'd gotten home, if I was mad at him. Nothing.

"Is this about Jodi?" Connor asked.

The muscles in my jaw tightened as I remembered her parting words in the bathroom.

Connor sighed, and I thought he might drop the subject, but instead, he said, "What should I have done? Kept dating her forever?"

I didn't answer.

Again he sighed, but this time he didn't say anything else.

"You don't have to be so rude to him all the time," Abbie said after we'd dropped off Connor and Chris.

I squeezed the steering wheel. "This is none of your business."

"You know, just because a guy isn't as hot as Eli doesn't mean you have to treat him like nothing."

When I laughed, it came out more bitter than I'd have liked. "Oh, are we airing grievances? If so, I'd like to discuss when you plan on telling Mom and Dad you're pregnant."

Abbie pursed her lips and didn't speak to me for the rest of the night, which suited me just fine.

Curtis tugged at Dad's old necktie strung through the belt loops of my jeans. "Skylar, my friend Mark came over this afternoon and Mom let me turn my room into a fort. You wanna see?"

Now Cameron pulled the bell sleeve of my sweater. "Me and Chris took Cevin for a walk after school and we saw a dead bird."

"Me and Mark played army until he had to leave for Cub Scouts."

"Its eye was missing. And there were ants on it."

"And we rushed our food. That's where you don't eat it all at once because you don't know how long it will be until you get new food."

"I think you mean rationed," I said. "You rationed your food."

"That's what I said."

"Well, guys, it sounds like you've had a very productive day."

Curtis cocked his head. "What does 'productive' mean?"

"That you got a lot done."

He considered this. "I've done my chores already. Cameron hasn't."

"Shut up," Cameron said.

"Cameron, we don't say that in this house," Amy said as she breezed into the living room. She adjusted an earring and smiled at me. "Thanks so much for doing this, honey."

"It's no problem," I said.

"Connor and Chris had planned to see that movie for so long, it would have broken my heart to make them miss it."

Cevin hopped onto my lap to investigate me. He attempted a lick of my face. Curtis erupted into giggles. "He likes you."

I rubbed his soft, white fur, hoping he wasn't about to pee on my lap. He wore the overeager expression that characterized the entire Ross family, as if whatever problems you brought into their house could be solved with affection and food.

Brian entered the living room as he tied his tie. "Do you think this one, honey, or the red one?"

Amy assessed him. "I like that one."

"Okay, good, because I don't want to go back upstairs." He turned to the couch. "You guys are going to be good for Skylar, right?"

"Yes," the two boys said, their voices angelic.

Brian said to me, "They've already watched their TV quota for the week, so unless Cameron wants to watch the news and find a current event for his school project, the TV needs to stay off. Amy made stuffed manicotti for you and put it in the fridge. All you need to do is pop it in the oven for a half hour. And there's ice cream bars in the basement freezer if you think they've earned it."

Impressive. When I was growing up, Dad never did the babysitter briefing. Even Mom's was sparse, consisting of the phone number for Pizza Hut, and how it took hours to calm Abbie down from caffeine, so please, please, please don't let her have any.

"Have a good time," I said as they moved toward the entry.

Brian tightened his tie. "I just hope his wife doesn't get drunk and puke on my shoes. That's what happened the last time my boss took out an employee."

Amy smiled at me. "Well, with a standard like that, I'm anticipating a great night." She beckoned Cameron and Curtis. "Come here, boys."

"No kisses, Mom, okay?" Cameron said. "You just put on lipstick."

"You mean like this?" Amy caught his forehead with her puckered mouth. Cameron let out a good-natured shriek and dove into my lap. With that, Amy and Brian left for the night.

I don't know which surprised me more, that I voluntarily gave up my Wednesday evening to watch two little boys, or that I enjoyed it. We held races in the backyard, we played Twister with the music cranked loud, and they declared me an honorary boy so I could enter Curtis's fort. After their baths, we ate ice cream bars and read a chapter from the book Brian brought out each night. When they coaxed a second chapter out of me, it happened because I wasn't ready yet for them to go to bed. Several pages into it, however, they drifted to sleep, so I closed the book and tiptoed to the door.

"Good night, Skylar," Cameron said in his drowsy-little-boy voice.

I switched off the light. "Good night."

Downstairs, I flipped through TV stations, but nothing held my interest. I turned it off as my cell phone sang with Lisa's call. I pushed her into voice mail. I couldn't handle any more whining about John and Alexis.

I stared at my silenced phone. Should I try Jodi again? Would it amount to anything? She hadn't said anything more to me than a crisp, "Hello," since she stormed from the bathroom on Monday. As if she had the right to be mad.

If anyone deserved to be angry, it was me. Her implying that I might date Connor . . . Well, it insulted me.

Sure, we'd become friends. Good friends, even. And he was cute, in a squirrelly kind of way. And yes, I'd noticed myself having some, well, warmish feelings toward him since he changed my tire, but it didn't matter. I'd never date him. Two of Jodi's exes in a row? How embarrassing.

Connor and Chris came through the front door at that moment, practically shouting about, of all things, pineapple in Dubai.

I rose from the couch. "Guys, shh. Your brothers are sleeping."

Connor froze. "What are you doing here?"

"What do you mean, what am I doing here? I'm babysitting."

"I didn't know Mom was calling you."

"Is there something wrong with my being here?"

"No, it just caught me off guard."

Silence followed. I tucked my bag over my shoulder. "I guess I don't need to be here now that you guys are home. I'll see you tomorrow morning."

"Tell Abbie hi for me." Chris followed this with a deep blush.

"I will." I nodded at Connor and walked through the door.

I had one leg in my car when Connor called, "Skylar, wait," from the front door. He jogged down the short path to the driveway. "I think we need to clear the air."

I retracted my leg and leaned against my car. "Do we?"

"Things have been really weird between us since Monday."

"Well, she's my best friend, and you're . . ." I could think of no good description. "You're someone I spend a lot of time with, so it's a little uncomfortable for me."

Connor nodded. "I know. But you understand why, right?"

"Why what?"

"Why I broke up with her. I assume Jodi talked to you about it."

I dug my toe into the ground. He already wanted to discuss this? They'd just broken up forty-eight hours ago. "We really shouldn't talk about it."

"But if we don't talk about it, then it becomes this thing we both know but neither of us says. I'd rather voice it so we can move on."

"You really think that's a good idea?"

He nodded. "Otherwise it'll keep getting weirder and we won't be able to stay friends."

"Fine." I shifted my weight and forced myself to hold eye contact. "Well, there's no good way to say this. I've done a lot of thinking about it, and it's not going to happen. I'm sorry."

Connor blinked several times. "What?"

I sighed. "Even if we ignore that I'm with Eli, you're Jodi's ex. You're sweet and funny, and I love your family, but—" I glared at him. "Okay, why are you smiling?"

Now he laughed. "Do you think I broke up with Jodi for you?"

My face warmed. "Okay, you don't have to laugh."

"Sorry." Connor bit his lip in an effort to dampen his smile. It didn't work. "It's just that you're such a good friend—"

I cut him off by raising my hand. "No need for further explanation."

"I didn't mean to offend you, it was just funny." Probably realizing how this sounded, he rushed to say, "Not that you aren't likable, because obviously you're . . . Well, you're Skylar. I think that pretty much sums it up."

I hurled my bag into the passenger seat. "I have to go."

"Don't be embarrassed."

"I'm not embarrassed," I said with the cool manner I'd perfected during my years of turning away eager boys. "I just have somewhere I need to be."

"Skylar," Connor attempted, but I drowned him out by turning my ignition key. Only one thing could make this situation more humiliating—Connor comforting me.

On the drive home, I held in tears for the first minute, then spent the second furious with myself. I couldn't fall apart because stupid Connor didn't want me for his girlfriend. Especially when I didn't even want to *be* his girlfriend.

I took several deep breaths before entering my house. "I'm not upset, I'm not upset," I said under my breath, then pushed open the garage door.

I found Mom seated in front of the TV. I perched beside her. "What are you watching?" After spending my evening in the Rosses' cozy living room, ours felt sterile.

She looked up from her magazine to the screen. "I'm not sure anymore. I haven't been paying attention."

It looked like a crime-fighting show—a guy and girl too good-looking to actually work for the FBI leaned over some hacked-up body. I knew it was fake but couldn't keep from making a face. "Mind if I turn it?"

"Please." She handed me the remote and returned to studying the pictures in her magazine. She turned it to me. "What do you think of this?"

I looked at a room dressed in silver and blue, full of twinkle lights and votive candles. "For what?"

Mom looked at me with exasperation. "You can't be serious. It's for your birthday party, Skylar."

"Oh, right." I flipped through the channels without absorbing anything. "It looks good."

Mom always got way into our birthday parties, but this year she seemed downright obsessed. She booked the country club back in the summer and had the invitations addressed and stamped, just waiting for Emily Post to say it was okay to mail them out.

She turned another page and made a "hmm" sound at whatever she saw there.

For some reason, I really wanted Mom to ask how my day was, how school had been, if any big tests were on the horizon. I wanted to feel like the woman seated beside me was my mom.

"Is Dad home?" I asked, even though his car wasn't in the garage.

"No."

"Is he at work?"

"I assume so. I haven't heard from him today."

"Why is he working so much more now?"

"Some big contract for the Sprint renovation. Skylar, honey, I'm trying to concentrate."

I turned back to the TV, where some bleached blonde chatted incessantly about her nails. Ugh. Didn't I get enough of that at school? I hit the power button.

"Fall Ball is the weekend after this," I informed Mom. "Eli Welling asked me today."

Not exactly true, but he'd bought our tickets that day at lunch. Apparently that was all the asking he'd intended to do.

When he'd returned to the table and I saw the tickets, I said, "You bought two?"

He smiled. "I thought you'd like one."

"Depends." I took a long drink from my water bottle, making him wait. "At the last thing you took me to, I had to find my own ride home."

Eli gave me a funny look. "Are you talking about James's?"

"Of course."

He blinked a couple times. "Are you mad at me?"

"Eli, you didn't even notice I left. Yeah, I'm a little annoyed."

"Of course I noticed. Connor talked to me about it."

"He did?" News to me.

"Yeah. He said you were ready to go home, and since he was sober, he'd drive you."

Connor had verified this later. Which meant I had no good reason to be mad at Eli or to skip Fall Ball. Unless Mom put her foot down, but she'd been pretty lenient about school dances in recent years, as long as we all went as a group.

Now, at the mention of Eli's name, Mom looked up. She never clocked off her job as boy patrol. "Has he expressed a romantic interest in you?"

"A romantic interest?" I smiled. "Mom, you sound so old when you phrase it like that. We'd be going as friends."

"In a group?"

"Of course."

She pressed her lips together. "And you wouldn't be alone with him at any point in the evening?"

"Nope."

"Then I suppose . . ." She sighed. "I suppose that'll be fine. I'll be seeing Cathy tomorrow at the women's tea, so I'll discuss it with her there. I want to make sure she's mindful of her son's intentions."

"Thank you," I said as Dad walked through the garage door. "Hi, Daddy."

"Was that you who left the door up again?"

"Oh, sorry."

"Sorry won't cut it when I walk out there one morning and find all our stuff gone. Not to mention what easy access it gives people to our house. I could have been a robber."

"Sorry," I repeated. "How was work?"

"Fine. The same." He hung his Windbreaker in the closet. "You two have already eaten, I assume?"

"I ate with the Rosses."

"Okay." He walked off toward the kitchen. No questions about why I would have eaten with the Rosses, or if Mom put leftovers in the fridge for him. In fact, he didn't acknowledge her at all.

I turned and found Mom engrossed once again by her magazine, but now her forehead creased as she gripped it, her knuckles bright white.

"I'm going upstairs to start on homework," I said.

She only nodded.

In my room, I didn't bother to turn on a light. I just sat on my bed and stared out the dark window from my dark house. Abbie's pop music bled through the walls, the peppy notes and sticky lyrics grating on me even more than normal. And finally, as the light, happy music clashed with the deep black inside me, the tears pushed through.

I rummaged through my desk drawer, finally finding what I wanted—the scrap of paper with Heather's cell phone number. She answered on the third ring.

"This is Skylar Hoyt," I said in a strained voice.

"Oh, Skylar." Her warmth only made me cry harder. "I haven't seen you at youth group. I've wondered about you."

I forced my tears into submission. "Are you praying for my family?"

"Of course," she said. "Did something else happen?"

"Nothing's happening."

I heard her hesitate. "It may feel that way, but in my experience, things are changing more than you can see."

But were they changing in the ways I wanted them to? I couldn't ask the question without sobbing, so I stayed quiet.

"Would you like to meet for coffee or something?" she asked.

"Please just keep praying," I said, and hung up.

9

Out of the blue, Eli said, "I'm thinking Italian."

"Italian?" Had I missed part of the phone conversation? Had I zoned out or something? "For what?"

"For Fall Ball. John and I thought we could split a limo, and my dad says there's a great Italian place downtown."

No way would my mom ever go for it. "Well, I need to ask my mom, but—"

"Need to ask me what?" Mom materialized in my doorway.

I jumped. "Oh, hi."

"Ask me what?"

"Plans for Fall Ball. John and Eli are talking about renting a limo and—"

Mom pursed her glossy lips. "Skylar, we talked about this. We agreed that you and your friends would get ready here and then you would meet Eli at the dance."

"I know, but I thought this would be okay since we're all going to the dance as a big group. All my girlfriends and their dates."

Mom considered this. "Will Connor be with you?"

"I'm not sure."

"See if Connor's going, and we'll talk."

"Okay."

"May I borrow your chandelier earrings?" she asked as she helped herself to my jewelry box. "I'm going out with some girlfriends tonight."

"Sure." When she'd taken the earrings and left, I said to Eli, "Okay, so my mom said—"

"Why'd you do that?" Eli asked, his voice dark.

"Do what?" But I had a good idea.

"Invite Connor out with us. The only reason we ever put up with him was Jodi, and she doesn't want him around."

"I didn't have a choice." I closed myself into my walk-in closet, just in case Mom happened to be nearby. "Please don't turn this into a big deal. She at least sounded open to the idea. That's what matters."

"What I don't understand"—he was really picking up steam now—"is how you have to hide our relationship, yet you can flaunt how friendly you are with Connor."

"I don't understand it either, but Mom loves Connor. She'll approve of anything if Connor's doing it—"

"Well, wonderful. How nice that your mom approves of the guy you're in love with."

The back of my neck tingled. His accusation felt far closer to the truth than I wanted. "That's just crazy."

"Well, he likes you. You know he does."

"Actually, I have it on pretty good authority that he doesn't."

Eli took a moment to process this. "What does that mean?"

"It means that Connor said he doesn't have feelings for me."

"And why would you guys be talking about that?"

I should have seen that coming. "It really doesn't matter."

"To your boyfriend it does."

I ran my hands through my hair. "I'm so sick of hearing you say stuff like that. We can't get through a single day without you reminding me that you're my boyfriend, that I'm your girlfriend, that we're together." I hesitated only a second. "Maybe we should've just stayed friends."

"If that's how you feel, fine." Then he hung up on me.

I swept my spoon along the edge of my ice cream cup. "At first it wasn't so bad, but now any time Connor's name comes up, he gets crazy."

"Oprah says that an absurdly jealous partner is often a sign that *they* are cheating," Alexis said. We all stared at her. "Oh! Not that I think Eli's cheating on you. What I meant is his jealousy is about him, not you."

"I, for one, can't believe he thinks you're into Connor," Lisa said with a dramatic roll of her eyes.

Jodi stabbed at her custard. "Maybe because she hangs out with him all the time."

I shot her a sharp look.

"I'm not saying *I* think you like him, but you are together an awful lot." She continued her stabbing. She'd done more stabbing than eating.

"Only because our parents are friends. How many times do I have to tell people that?"

"So what's the deal?" Lisa asked. She appeared deeply concerned. She hadn't snarled at Alexis even once since we arrived. "Did you guys break up?"

"I don't know. We hung up on each other before making it clear."

"Do you want to break up with him?"

I took a big bite of custard as I thought about this. "I don't want him to be jealous."

"Take it from me, that's impossible for Eli," Jodi said. "You just have to decide if it's worth putting up with."

They all paused eating to stare at me, breath baited.

"Well." I allowed another bite to melt in my mouth. "I don't want to spend my last year of high school battling with him."

At first, no one spoke, then Alexis rested a hand on my shoulder.

"On Oprah a couple weeks ago"—I should have expected this—"she had on this group of women who'd given up something important in high school for a boy. It was so inspiring. You should come over and watch it."

Thankfully, Lisa interrupted Oprah hour. "Okay, this is why Eli is crazy." Her gaze was fixed beyond me, and we turned to see a group of three guys waiting for their order. When we looked at them, they looked away. "The really cute one in the green shirt has been staring at you ever since he arrived."

Alexis twirled dark hair onto her finger as she evaluated the boys. "When you look at a group of guys like that, do you ever wonder if maybe one of them is *the* guy?"

I laughed. "No, not ever."

"I do," Jodi said, her voice just as dreamy as Alexis's. "And sometimes I wonder how it might affect my life if I talk to him. Like maybe I'd fall in love and change all my college plans so we could be together. Or maybe he knows a modeling agent."

"Or maybe," I said, "you'd discover he's just like every other guy you already know."

Jodi smiled at me, the new smile she'd used since the summer, where her lips curled but her eyes remained flat. "You're awful bitter when you and Eli fight." She looked at the guys again, who now walked away from the window with their ice cream. "Hey!" she called.

"Jodi," Alexis hissed. Lisa giggled and blushed, but I just watched, amused.

"Hey!" Jodi yelled again, this time drawing their attention to our spot on the grassy slope. "There's room over here for you guys!"

The three of them froze there for a moment, as if shocked by her brazen offer. Green Shirt spoke first. "Cool, thanks."

"I can't believe you just did that," Alexis whispered, her voice filled with admiration.

Jodi shrugged and smiled. "I'm not passing up a potential modeling contract."

Jodi and Lisa—the two single ones—scooted apart to make room for them.

"I'm Nick," Green Shirt said as he took a seat. "This is Brett and Patrick."

Brett and Patrick were good-looking in a nondescript kind of way, brown hair and eyes. Nick, with his broad shoulders and dark curls, was definitely the pick of the group, which didn't go unnoticed by Jodi. As she pressed them for information—Where do you go to school? Have you always been in private schools?—her eyes stayed locked on Nick.

"So what brought you up this way?" she asked after learning how far out in the suburbs they lived.

"Brett just got dumped by his girlfriend." Nick seemed the only one capable of talking. "We went out cruising and wound up here." Inexplicably, he winked at me.

"We think Skylar just got dumped too," Lisa said.

"We brought her out to get her mind off it." Jodi offered me a faux-sympathetic smile, like the ice cream run was her idea. *I* had invited *her*.

Now Nick smiled at me, except his wasn't fake. "Something tells me you'll make a quick recovery."

I looked away, unwilling to indulge his flirting. Besides him being too eager for my taste, I possibly had a boyfriend.

My phone rang from the middle of the circle, where Alexis had placed it so we could laugh every time Eli called. She leaned to look at the caller ID. "Yep, it's him again."

"I take it you're not answering." Nick winked at me again. Okay, that was annoying.

"He's called four times in the last"—Lisa consulted the clock on my cell phone—"twelve minutes." She giggled, her clear eyes fixed on Brett, the dumpee, staying true to her sickness for guys on the rebound.

"Come on, Skylar," Nick said, as if we were old friends. "He's trying so hard."

I kept my gaze on my ice cream. "He should've tried harder sooner."

Nick recognized me then as the girl with a moat, stone wall, and iron gate built around her heart. That was all it took for him to dedicate his relentless attention on winning me over, the way numerous guys had before him.

As the night darkened, so did Jodi's mood. This was the same old story with us, my unintentionally stealing a guy by being difficult. So I'd been right—Nick, Brett, and Patrick were exactly like every other guy she already knew. The only one who'd been different had just dumped her.

At the end of the night, Nick pressed an old Best Buy receipt into my hand. He'd scribbled his phone number on the back.

"What a shock," Jodi said as I climbed into Lisa's Wrangler.

"You want it?" I tossed it onto her lap. "Be my guest."

She wiped it off her bare legs like a burning coal. With a quick exhale of disgust, she turned from me.

Abbie slid open the pocket door. "Eli called for you twice."

I jammed the toothbrush around my mouth with too much force. I'd forbidden Eli to call the house line in case Mom picked up. "What did he say?"

"He asked where you were and I said I didn't know. Then he asked if you were with Connor. I said yes, even though I knew you weren't."

I spit. "You should've told him the truth."

"The second time he called"—I caught her eyes gleaming and knew this wouldn't be good—"I told him you died."

"Abbie!"

"I even cried. It was great."

"What's wrong with you?"

She shrugged. "I was just having fun with him."

"It can't always be about fun."

Abbie narrowed her eyes and jabbed at her stomach.

"You think I don't know that?" She rolled the door closed with a bang.

Connor eyed my new boots. "Those are some serious shoes."

"Thanks." I grinned down at them. They were creamy black leather with squared-off toes and made a great, authoritative sound as we walked to our lockers.

"You should add some fishnets so you can really capture the hooker look."

I rolled my eyes. "There's nothing wrong with my boots. You just have no sense of style. They're very in right now."

Ever since my misinterpretation of his breakup with Jodi, both of us had gone to great lengths to point out each other's flaws.

"In or out, they're stupid. Why do your legs need shoes? That's what pants were invented for."

"When shoes are this cute"—I paused to lift one in the air—"it doesn't matter if they make sense."

We turned down our locker row and found Eli leaning against my locker, talking to Alexis.

Eli stopped midsentence. "Hi."

"Hey," I said.

Alexis grabbed her backpack. "I have to go to the bathroom."

"I just realized I already have my book." Connor backed up a few steps. "See you guys in class."

We watched them leave, then looked at each other warily, unsure of who should make the first move.

"So." Eli scratched the scruff of his chin. "They thought

you were a goner but managed to revive you on the operating table, huh?"

His tone allowed me a slight smile. "Sorry about that. Little sisters, you know."

"I'm the youngest, so actually I don't."

"Oh, well, you younger siblings are pains sometimes." He looked unsure of how to take this, so I rushed on. "About last night—"

"I was out of line," Eli interrupted.

I'd been about to launch into reasons why I didn't think we should see each other anymore. Now I just stood there and stared at him.

"I get frustrated by how secretive we have to be, that's all." Eli reached for my hand and I allowed him to entwine our fingers. "I wish I could come to your house, pick you up, and take you out. I shouldn't have taken my frustrations out on you. I'm sorry."

Looking at him, at his ocean-colored eyes and perfect face, I wanted this to work. On paper we made a perfect match. Why couldn't my heart get with the program and fall for this guy? Why did I keep getting tripped up by stupid Connor Ross? Here Eli had saved me from a horrendous night, and what had Connor done but laugh in my face at the thought of him having a crush on me? I owed Eli another chance.

"I guess I was a little inconsiderate of your feelings," I said.

"So." Eli swung my hand, his eyes crinkling with a faint smile. "Fight over?"

"Fight over," I agreed.

10

Jodi tied a ribbon into her ponytail with so much force I thought it might rip. "It's high school etiquette at the most basic level. You don't dump someone so close to a dance. You wait until the day after."

I wound my hair up off my neck, then leaned to examine it in the mirror. "There's no convenient time for a breakup."

"Oh, how would you know?" Jodi snapped. "You've never been through one."

Silence filled the room. This rift between Jodi and me, subtle at first, had escalated these last two weeks, tainting any time we spent together. We'd suddenly become an awkward group, Jodi versus me and Lisa versus Alexis.

Except Alexis and Lisa appeared to have called a truce on their bickering. They weren't friendly toward each other by any stretch of the word, but they limited themselves to eye rolling and muttering under their breath. If the whole John thing had happened sophomore year, or even junior year, one of them would've left the group. Probably Alexis. But no one wanted to find a new group of friends senior year.

Although with the looks Jodi had been shooting me all

night, maybe there were worse things than finding new friends.

Sensing the discomfort she'd invited, Jodi turned on her penitential voice. "I'm sorry, Skylar. I'm just going through a rough time. I don't mean to take it out on you."

I avoided eye contact and continued pinning my hair. "It's fine."

"Why don't you and I skip the dance?" Lisa suggested as she completed drawing her cat whiskers. This year the money raised at Fall Ball went to the drama club, so dress code was "whimsical formal," which left much open to interpretation. Most guys intended to wear tuxes and come as James Bond, while us girls recycled prom dresses and threw on butterfly wings or cat ears.

"Skip the dance?" Alexis gave them an incredulous look. "You can't skip the dance. You'll miss everything."

"What's to miss about going to a dance alone? It's so pathetic." Apparently realizing what she'd just said, Jodi hurried to add, "What I mean is, it's fine for you, Lisa, but Connor and I just broke up."

"At least he doesn't have a date." Lisa adjusted the straps of her dress. "John'll be there with another girl."

Alexis narrowed her eyes but didn't respond.

"You should come to the dance, Jodi," I said.

"Skylar's right." Alexis sat beside Jodi. "Is 'I'm defeated' the message you want to send the world?" She tilted her head the way she'd seen Oprah do on TV. "Do you really want to give Connor the satisfaction of not going because of him?"

"If anybody should stay home, it's Connor." Lisa pressed her lips together to even the lip gloss, then separated them with a loud smack.

"Maybe he won't come," I said. "He's not exactly the type who loves to dress up."

"Oh, he'll be there." Jodi rolled her eyes. "With 'whimsical formal,' he figures he can get away with track pants."

Lisa gasped at the horror.

Alexis's eyes widened. "He wouldn't."

Jodi shrugged and offered a smile, soft with nostalgia. "You know, his clothes used to really bother me, but not now. Now it seems kind of cute."

I paused my mascara application midstroke. Jodi had spoken my exact thoughts.

"I can't go." She plucked at her skirt. "This dress is all wrong."

Enough was enough. I chucked a lipstick tube at her. "You're coming and you know it."

"Ow!" Jodi massaged her bicep. "That really hurt."

"Grab one of my formals and paint on some whiskers."

"I can't fit into your dresses." She clutched my pillow to her chest and moped into it. "I'm too fat."

"You're a size smaller than me."

"No I'm not," she said, as if dress sizes were mere opinion rather than actual numbers.

"Try this one." I tossed my silver dress at her, the one I wore to prom with a sleazebag senior. "I can hardly breathe in it, so it should fit you fine."

Good thing we'd decided not to do the limo thing with the guys and just meet them at the dance. Persuading Jodi into the formal took fifteen minutes. Lots of, "No, you don't want to go home and change into your pj's," and, "What? You think you've gained weight? We were all just saying it looks like you've *lost* weight." Doing her makeup and getting her in the car took another half hour.

When we finally arrived at the school, the girls dragged Jodi toward the gymnasium and I headed the opposite direction. I couldn't take her self-pity for another second. If she asked me one more time if I thought her hips had "filled out," I might say yes just to break the monotony.

I went to the refreshment room, a classroom where they kept sodas and snacks for those exhausted from dancing. I found Connor there, surveying his drink options.

I planted my hands on my hips. "Thank you oh-so-much for such a delightful evening."

He didn't look up from the table. "What are you talking about?"

"Jodi is driving me crazy."

"How's that—" He looked at me. "Wow, you look great. What are you?"

"Hello?" I clicked my plastic shoes together. "Light blue dress? Glass slippers? I'm Cinderella."

"Are those really glass? I mean, I know your dad is crazy rich, but . . ."

"I found them at the Disney Store. They're killing my feet. I can't imagine what actual glass slippers would feel like."

"Fortunately, I can't sympathize." Connor wiggled a sneakered foot at me. "I'm so comfortable it's like I'm not even at a dance."

I wrinkled my nose. "You look like you're headed to the gym."

"Weren't you about to yell at me for something?" he asked, popping open a Dr Pepper.

"Yes, why would you—" He handed the soda to me. "Oh, thank you. Why would you break up with Jodi right before a dance?"

Connor blinked at me several times, the way he did when trying to untangle the meaning of my words. "It honestly didn't cross my mind."

"It's common courtesy."

"If I waited until after, it would have been too close to something else." He shrugged, as if to suggest he didn't control the timing of these things. "There's really no convenient time to break up with someone."

"But do you realize what I've gone through tonight?" I stole a pretzel from his stash. "Just getting her in the car took fifteen minutes."

Connor smiled. "I should've guessed—this is about you."

I grinned back. "Is there something wrong with that?"

"I'm used to it, actually. It just helps me to know that, while it's about Jodi, this conversation isn't *really* about Jodi."

I opened my mouth to respond, but Jodi barged into the conversation.

"There you are." She grabbed my arm as if everything was still hunky-dory between us. "I've been looking *everywhere* for you. Did you see who I was just dancing with?"

"No, I didn't." I transferred my Dr Pepper to the other hand so she didn't spill it with all her jostling.

She smiled at Connor. "Oh, hi." As if she just noticed him. As if he wasn't the real reason she burst in here.

Connor failed to hide his amused smile. "Hey, Jodi."

"Nice pants." Then she pulled me toward the door. "Eli's looking for you."

I glanced over my shoulder at Connor and mouthed "Sorry." He winked and turned his attention to a cookie platter.

"What's wrong with you?" Jodi hissed as she yanked me down the hall to some unknown destination. "You knew I didn't want to come tonight because of Connor, and then I find you yakking the night away with him."

"We weren't yakking," I said. "And could you ease up on my arm? You're giving me a bruise." She relaxed her grip enough for me to pull away. "I was actually getting onto Connor for dumping you like he did."

Jodi cast me a suspicious eye. "You were?"

"Of course." She kept looking at me like I'd done something wrong, so I added, "What on earth would he and I have to talk about outside of you?"

She smiled and shook her head. "What's wrong with me these days? I never should've doubted you." She looped her arm through mine. "Stupid Eli, making me all paranoid."

My stomach tightened the way it often did when his name arose between us. "What did Eli say?"

"Oh, we were talking the other night about you and Connor, how often you guys seem to be thrown together." She followed this with another shake of her head, as if to convey what a not-big deal it was. "He said something about how you would probably side with Connor over the breakup, since—"

"I didn't know you two even talked." I couldn't process anything beyond her first few words.

"Of course we talk. I see him every day."

"What I meant is, I didn't know you guys talked at night. One-on-one. About Connor and me."

She looked confused. "Eli and I are good friends, Skylar. You know that."

Did I?

But before I could ask anything else, she squeezed my arm. "C'mon. I just met this really cute junior."

And though we left the hallway, I didn't leave my questions.

"Would you say you and Jodi are good friends?" I asked as Eli held me close for a slow dance.

He pulled back to look at me. "What'd you say?"

"You and Jodi. Would you say you're good friends?"

He laughed, but it seemed forced. "Skylar, I know you don't have any experience with this, but it's a turnoff to have your ex brought up at a time like this."

"I'm curious. Do you and Jodi talk much?"

"You're very cute when you're jealous." He kissed my forehead. "You know you don't need to be."

"I'm not jealous, I'm curious. She said you guys are 'good friends,' but I've never gotten that impression from you, so I'm wondering"—I sucked in a breath and met his eyes—"how good of friends are you?"

He studied my face for a moment. "What's wrong with me being good friends with Jodi? You're friends with Connor. Isn't it the same thing?"

"He's not my ex-boyfriend."

"Is that what this is about? I don't even think of Jodi being my ex-girlfriend. She's just Jodi."

I narrowed my eyes. "Except you just told me it was a turnoff having her—your ex—brought up while we're dancing."

"What I meant is, it's a turnoff talking about *anyone* when we're dancing. I just want it to be you and me." He brushed wisps of bangs from my face. "And it shouldn't matter if I'm friends with Jodi, because you know I love *you*."

Then he swallowed as he awaited my response.

I understood the delicacies of this moment, that there were expectations, but I couldn't make myself answer. I just stood there like a moron and stared at him.

Finally, Eli pulled me against him where he couldn't see me speechless.

"Teri?" Dad called.

"No, it's Skylar." I left my Cinderella shoes in the entry and followed Dad's voice to the kitchen. He sat at the counter with a pile of receipts, the checkbook, and a glass of red wine. "Bills on a Saturday night?"

He glanced at me over the top of his glasses. "Unfortunately, yes."

I took the stool next to him. My eyes caught on a party rentals invoice. $5,092.73. Yowzer. "Who's having a party?"

Dad raised an eyebrow. "You."

"Oh. Right."

A long silence ensued. I picked at my nail polish, unsure of how to gracefully leave. As I opened my mouth to fake yawn and claim exhaustion, Dad asked, "Did you have a good time at the dance?"

"Yeah," I lied. My feet swung slightly, bumping against the counter.

"Please don't do that."

I stopped. Instinctively, my feet searched for one of the stool's horizontal bars, but they groped in vain. These were new. Mom threw out the others last week. "Where's Mom?"

"Out with some friends."

"Where'd they go?"

"I think the Melting Pot. Or maybe that was last week. I don't know."

"Oh."

Another silence. I asked the only thing I could ever think to ask my father. "How's work?"

"Oh, stressful. Nothing new." He shrugged, as if work, this thing that sucked up all his time, was unimportant.

"Did you win the jazz district renovation?"

Dad looked up from the register and blinked at me for a few seconds. "How did you know about that?"

"You mentioned it at dinner a couple nights ago."

"Oh." The corners of his mouth turned up. "Yes, we did."

I smiled. "That's great."

"It is." He nodded, as if approving of me. "Thank you, Skylar."

It seemed like a good time to leave, with both of us feeling good about the conversation, but before I made my excuses, Dad's face turned serious. "I'm worried about your sister."

I traced the swirling pattern of Mom's granite countertop. "What about her?"

"Why wasn't she at the dance tonight? That doesn't seem like Abbie."

"I don't know." Could he tell I'd broken out in a sweat? "You'll have to ask her."

"I did. She told me she didn't feel well and went to bed around eight."

I shrugged. "There you go."

Dad shook his head. "But it doesn't make sense. I can't remember Abbie ever having plans to go."

"Well, you've been working a lot." Annoyance seeped into my voice. With all the hours he worked, did he really expect he wouldn't miss things at home?

Dad noted my tone and bent over the register. "I need to get back to this."

"Fine." I hopped down from my stool. "Good night, Dad."

He held a receipt up to the light, studying it. "Good night."

I trudged upstairs, sticky and sore from the dance. What a lousy night. How come supposedly fun activities—parties, dances—didn't feel fun anymore? I should've faked sick and stayed home too.

But as I cleaned up for bed, it occurred to me that maybe Abbie hadn't faked. Maybe she really didn't feel good.

"Abbie?" I whispered, followed by a gentle rap on the pocket door. "You okay?"

Silence.

I hesitated, not wanting to wake her. I pushed open the door a crack. "Abbie?"

Still nothing. Not even breathing.

I slid the door open until the band of light finally hit her bed, revealing she wasn't in it.

11

A little after 1:30, I heard Abbie sneak up the stairs. She tiptoed into her bedroom, closed the door with a soft click, and exhaled with relief.

"Nice to see you," I said.

Abbie faced me, a hand over her heart. "This isn't what it looks like."

"So you're *not* sneaking into the house at"—I glanced at her alarm clock—"1:43?"

"I am, but I wasn't doing anything bad."

I stood from her bed. "I've been lying here worrying about you for the last couple hours. Why didn't you take your cell phone?"

"I wasn't thinking clearly." Abbie chewed on her lip for a moment. "I didn't mean to make you worry."

I crossed my arms over my chest. "Where were you? I didn't see you at the dance."

"I didn't go. I really didn't plan to leave the house tonight, but then . . ."

"Then what?"

"Chris—"

"Abbie." I rubbed my dry eyes. "Now is really not the time for someone like Chris."

"I can't help it. And we weren't doing anything bad. Well, other than sneaking out, I guess. We just went to the park and sat and talked." She followed me through the bathroom and into my room. "I know I probably shouldn't have, but he's just so great, and—"

I turned and faced her. "Have you told him?"

She averted her eyes. "No."

"Is that really fair? Making him think this is leading somewhere it can't?"

"But why can't it?" Abbie nearly whimpered.

"Abbie, you're pregnant."

"But—"

"But nothing. Yes, Chris likes you a lot, but no fifteen-year-old guy is going to stick it out with you when he finds out you're pregnant from your last relationship."

Abbie looked to the floor, deflated. Her silence lasted so long I nearly asked her to leave.

"If any guy would support me," she whispered, "I think it would be him."

Then she turned and left, sliding the door shut before I had a chance to agree.

"You weren't at church this morning," Connor said when I answered my phone.

"No, I wasn't." I snapped off the light of my new sewing machine. This sewing thing had taken a couple weeks, but I was finally getting the hang of it. "Late night around here."

"Oh, right. Jodi's."

"Jodi's?"

"Didn't you all get together at Jodi's?"

I snipped a thread. "No."

"I thought I overheard Alexis and Jodi talking about some kind of after party."

"You must have heard wrong." But somehow, I knew he hadn't. I had a strange sensation deep inside my chest, an itchiness. Was that how it felt when you suspected being left out?

"Anyway," Connor continued, as if my group of friends ousting me was trivial, "I just heard on the radio that this is supposedly one of our last warm days of the year. Chris and I are hitting Sheridan's. You and Abbie wanna come?"

I hesitated. "I think Abbie might have homework."

"Just check with her," Connor said. "We don't have to be gone long."

What else could I do? I had to ask and hope that what I'd said the night before would make Abbie proceed with caution for once in her life.

Instead, she said, "Sounds good," and rolled off her bed, where she'd been scribbling in a notebook.

"Really?" I gave her a look. "You don't have homework or anything?"

Her eyes remained locked to mine. "I have it under control."

I exhaled nice and slow to leave her doubtless of my disapproval, then said to Connor, "We'll both go."

"Great," Connor said. "You don't need to run this by your mom or anything? I know I have that scary Y chromosome."

"You have what?" I asked, distracted by Abbie rifling through her closet for something different to wear.

"A Y chromosome. As opposed to an X. Meaning that I'm a boy." He sighed at my silence. "It was a joke, Skylar."

"Well, Mom won't care. For some reason she's taken to you and Chris, X chromosomes or not."

"No, I have a *Y* chromosome. Girls have—" Connor stopped. "Never mind. I'll pick you up in a couple minutes."

Now off the phone, I stood in Abbie's room and watched her pull several skirts from her closet.

"Stop it." She didn't even turn around. "This is none of your business."

"Fine," I muttered as I left.

In the car, I hardly heard a word Connor spoke. Abbie and Chris's conversation distracted me—light, easy banter with a hint of flirtation.

Connor waved a hand in front of my face. "Are you even listening to me?"

"Yes." I punched the word. "You were talking about Mr. Huntley."

He rolled his eyes. "That was five minutes ago. What's wrong with you today? You seem off."

"I'm fine."

"Are you?"

"Yes. Honestly."

"Sure you are. That's why you haven't noticed we're not in my mom's minivan."

I looked at my surroundings, all gray leather and spotless carpet. And there was a distinct smell, same as Eli's Land Rover the morning after Jodi's party. "Did you get a new car?"

"Wow. Tell me you plan to pursue a career as a PI."

I slugged him in the arm. "When did you get this? What is it?"

"A Chevy Tahoe. We picked it up yesterday."

"It's great. Very . . ." I swept my gaze across the console, full of lights and buttons and switches. "Very macho."

"And therefore perfect for me, right?" Connor flexed one of his skinny arms. "Now you don't always have to take us to school. We can take you too."

I forgot to respond because in the seat behind me, Abbie giggled at something Chris said.

"Skylar?" Connor said. "Seriously. What's wrong with you?"

"Nothing."

"Problems with Eli? I notice your phone hasn't rung in the last ten minutes. That can't be a good sign."

I forced a laugh, remembering the hurt in Eli's eyes last night when I didn't say the expected, "I love you too." What would happen now? Could a relationship survive when one person said, "I love you," and the other stood there wishing he hadn't?

"Well, this should be a fun outing," Connor said as he turned into Sheridan's lot. "I can't get a word out of you."

I shook my head. "I'll be better, I promise."

Later, as we settled onto the grass between Sheridan's and the road, Connor asked, "Is it Eli stuff or other stuff that's bothering you?"

"It's all kinds of things." I glanced at Abbie and Chris. They opted for a bench near the parking lot because Abbie didn't want to sit on the grass in her skirt.

"Like what?"

I made myself turn away from his brother and my sister. "Was Eli at church this morning?"

Connor blinked a few times before answering, appearing confused by my answering his question with a question of my own. "I saw his parents but not him. Why?"

"Just curious." I stabbed at my custard a couple times. It shouldn't bother me. I'd been MIA as well. "He hasn't been there the last couple Sundays, but that's okay, right?"

Connor's forehead creased. "Why are you asking me?"

"You've been doing this a lot longer than me. I just wondered about your opinion."

"I've been doing what longer than you?"

"Church. Well, not church, because I've done that most my life. But religion. You have more experience."

Connor relaxed on his elbows and studied me. "What do you mean by religion?" He almost sounded offended.

"Like doing what they say to do in church. No swearing, no drinking. That kind of stuff."

"You don't drink."

"Yeah, well." I chuckled. "That hasn't always been the case."

"Funny you should mention that." Connor paused and stirred his hot fudge sundae.

"Mention what? Drinking?"

He met my gaze. When the sun hit his face like that, his eyes looked green. "Jodi told me you were a real wild girl, but all of a sudden you stopped wanting to have fun." He smiled. "Well, those were her words. I assume what she means is you pass on Jell-O shots."

"That's pretty accurate." I took a big bite of my ice cream, making it clear I had no plans of expanding my statement.

"Fine. I'll just ask." He leaned toward me. "What made

you go from a wild girl to worrying about if your boyfriend was at church?"

Aaron's face floated in front of me, handsome and inviting. Too handsome and inviting.

"Just . . ." How to explain without really explaining? "Just a bad experience."

I forced myself to look at Connor. His face showed disappointment.

"You know I'm not one of your silly girlfriends." I'd never heard him sound so angry. "I've got no intentions of talking about you behind your back or using what you say as blackmail. Haven't I proven that to you by now?"

My response came out as a whisper. "Yeah."

He looked at me with hard, challenging eyes. "Then why don't you ever share anything real with me?"

"You know more real things about me than anyone. Even Eli." I glanced at him. He looked doubtful. "It's not easy for me. The vulnerability thing."

Connor poked around his sundae, appearing pensive, and a long silence ensued.

Finally, I couldn't take it any longer. "We had this deal, Eli and me. Something happened, something big, and I knew it was time for a life change. I told Eli I wanted to go back to church and stop partying and stuff. He said he would do it with me."

"And is he?" Connor kept his voice soft, as if he feared spooking me.

I hesitated. "Sometimes."

"You said he dragged you to James's party. That doesn't sound very supportive to me."

"That wasn't his fault."

"How?"

I focused unblinking eyes on my ice cream, hoping I wouldn't have to suffer the humiliation of crying in front of Connor. Again. "I was weak. I should have said no."

"Why do you stay with him?"

I studied him. "What do you mean?"

"You don't like him. I can tell."

"That's not true."

"Oh, you like the *idea* of him, but really, Eli drives you crazy." He tilted his head, like a puppy trying to understand. "Why do you continue with him? Because he's popular?"

I hadn't been this offended since he'd called me a cliché. "That has nothing to do with it."

Connor snorted. "So you like guys with anger management issues who flirt with all your friends when you're not looking?"

Normally I was a pro at mastering my emotions, at turning on a chilly voice, but for some reason I couldn't this time. I sputtered like a pot ready to boil over. "Eli and I are absolutely none of your business!"

He lifted his shoulders, unflappable as always. "Maybe not, but as your best friend I'm concerned by how I see him treating you."

A response sat on the tip of my tongue, just waiting to shoot Connor's direction, but those two words adjusted priorities. "Best friend?" I laughed. "You're not my best friend."

"Oh yes I am."

"No you're not, and I get more of a say in it than you do."

"None of those girls are willing to tell you what you need

to hear"—he pointed his spoon at me—"which is that Eli is the wrong guy for you."

Of course, this thought had bounced around in my head since that night at QuikTrip, but it'd never been spoken, never been made subject to discussion.

I laughed again, but this time I forced it. "So, because you're nosy and have a big mouth, you're my best friend?"

"That's right."

"Jodi is—"

"Not your friend at all," he finished for me. "Trust me."

I burned with shame imagining what he'd seen that made him say that. Jodi bad-mouthing me. Hosting parties and leaving my name off the invite list. Maybe even plotting revenge.

"Jodi's been my best friend since eighth grade." What did I hope to convince him of by saying that?

Connor evaluated me. "You know she's mad at you."

"Of course I know." I took to jabbing at my ice cream rather than eating. "Don't you think I would fix it if I could?"

"It's practically all she talks about, your betrayal. She's obsessed. It's why we're not together anymore."

My heart pounded so loud, I feared he could hear it. "Because she won't talk about anything else?"

He shook his head. "Because she's always talking trash about you. At first I didn't care as much as I should have. But now . . ." Connor turned to me, squinting in the glare of the sun. "Well, we're friends now." He grinned. "Best friends."

I thought about these last couple months, how Connor

had spoken more truth about my life than Jodi had in the last five years. Here I'd assumed I had a crush on him, but maybe I was just experiencing my first real friend. This comforted me. I didn't want to date someone who owned such a variety of running pants.

"We're not going to, like, exchange friendship bracelets or anything, are we?"

He snorted. "Please, no." He plucked the thick, beaded bracelet decorating my wrist. "I can only imagine what kind of wacky, zebra-print contraption you'd invent for me."

I laughed and returned to my ice cream, now a souplike consistency. The breeze blew cool on my face, reminding me to enjoy the warm sun while I could. "What a beautiful day. Thanks for inviting me out."

"Well, I can't take credit. It was Chris's idea to call you girls."

"Really." I glanced over my shoulder and caught Chris winding his fingers through Abbie's. "So, what do you think of Chris and Abbie?"

"How do you mean?" he asked around a bite of ice cream.

"About them dating."

His eyes widened. "They're dating?"

I nodded in their direction. "See for yourself."

He fixed his gaze on them. "I had no idea. How long has this been going on?"

"I think since we had dinner at your house. You really didn't know?"

Connor shook his head.

"Stop staring," I said, and he turned his wide eyes back to me. "I don't know what to do. I told Abbie she needed to tell Chris about"—I forced myself to speak it—"the baby, but she still hasn't told our parents yet."

"What's she waiting for?"

"I don't know. Courage, I guess."

Connor shook his head and resumed blinking and breathing as normal. "You think she'll tell them soon?"

"She doesn't have much of a choice. She'll start showing before long."

Connor didn't say anything, just fixed his gaze on his ice cream and stirred with slow strokes.

Monday morning when I arrived at school, sans Connor for once because of a dentist appointment, I found only Eli at our group of lockers.

"Good morning." He touched my forehead with his lips. "How are you?"

It startled me how normal he behaved. "Fine. How are you?"

"Great. Sorry I wasn't at church yesterday." He offered a sheepish grin. "I overslept."

"That's okay." I searched his face for clues that things had shifted between us.

Eli laughed. "You're making me nervous."

I shook my head and forced a smile. "Sorry. Just . . . zoning out, I guess."

He leaned against the locker and watched me spin in my combination. "So, your party invitation arrived."

"Oh yeah?"

"I guess it came on Friday, but Mom didn't give it to me until yesterday. Looks fancy."

"Well, you know my mom," I said with an eye roll. "Every day when I get home from school she's asking me questions like, 'How about cilantro potatoes and beef satay?'"

"What's beef satay?"

"Some Indonesian dish, I think. I don't know." I folded the flap of my bag and closed my locker.

Eli fit an arm around my waist. "You ready to go?"

"Sure." I kept my eyes on his face as we walked down the hall. He really did seem okay. Was it possible, or was this an act?

Eli laughed again. "Why do you keep looking at me like that? I feel like I'm under the microscope this morning."

"No reason," I said, and turned away. Apparently, I worried for nothing.

Lisa rolled her eyes. "What's the big deal? Just say it already."

"What's the big deal?" I gave her an incredulous look, at which Lisa shrugged. "'I love you' is one of the most serious things you can say to another person."

"Oh, Skylar." She sighed and returned to her biology reading.

"It's a big deal," I insisted.

"It's not like it's your virginity," Lisa said too loud for our classroom setting. The guy seated across from us raised an eyebrow.

"Shh," I hissed.

She lowered her voice. "All I'm saying is, it's not going to drastically alter your relationship."

I chewed my lip as I considered this. How could it not

change things? I suspected Lisa could be wrong about this. "Did you tell John you loved him?"

"Of course."

Had that been such a dumb question? "Why 'of course'?"

"We were together for nearly a year. There are certain things that happen in that amount of time."

I tapped my pencil against my textbook. "Had you said it after four months?"

"We got together in January and said it Valentine's Day."

"You both said it? Like in cards or something?"

"No, at dinner. He said it first, then I said it back." She tilted her book toward me and pointed to a fungus picture. "That's disgusting."

"Did you mean it when you said it?"

Lisa sighed. "I don't know. I don't remember."

"What about now? Do you regret it?"

Lisa narrowed her eyes, as if debating whether she should be offended. "What kind of question is that?"

"I'm just trying to sort this thing out."

"Look, Skylar." She folded her arms over her book. "I don't know for sure, but I still think I loved John back then. Maybe in college I'll meet someone new and realize that I was wrong, that what I thought was love really wasn't. But then maybe later I'll meet someone else and think the same thing about *that* guy." She patted my hand, seeming to sense my discouragement. "My point is, you can't overthink it or you'll drive yourself crazy. Just tell Eli you love him. It's time to get over being scared."

"I'm not scared."

“Then what’s the problem?”

I scratched at a stain on my pants, a drip of ice cream from my afternoon with Connor. I chose not to answer Lisa’s question. Instead, I asked my own. “Did Jodi have a party after Fall Ball?”

“What? No. Of course not.” She followed her denials with a laugh. “Don’t you think you would’ve been invited if she had?”

“I’d have thought so,” I said. “But recently it feels like Jodi wants me out.”

It happened too quickly to know for sure, but I swear I saw a flicker of fear in Lisa’s bright eyes.

12

"I'm thinking up," Abbie said as she twisted my hair off my neck. "And dramatic eyes, but just touches of makeup everywhere else."

I fussed with the skirt of my yellow silk dress as Abbie tucked pins into my hair. "You know, it's not like I'm a bride or anything."

"You're the lady of the evening. Now shut up and let me have my fun."

Abbie did my makeup twice and my hair three times. The first hairstyle didn't seem elegant enough to her, but the second looked too over-the-top, so she redid it the first way. I'd never been more grateful to hear Connor knock on the door.

Abbie spritzed herself with perfume. "Tell them I'll be right down."

"Don't take too long." I slipped into the coat Mom bought to match my dress. "Mom won't like me being late to my own birthday party."

"I'm right behind you," she said, but since she was raking through her makeup bag, I wasn't so sure.

Downstairs, I pulled open the front door to find Connor and Chris looking uncomfortable in creased pants and collars. "My rescuers have arrived."

Chris laughed as he entered. "What are we rescuing you from?"

"Your girlfriend. She's been fussing with me for forty-five minutes now."

"Where is she?" he asked with an amused smile.

"Upstairs. She'll be down in a couple minutes." I glanced at Connor, but he looked away. I opened my mouth to ask what was wrong when Abbie thundered down the stairs.

"Sorry, sorry, sorry." She gave Chris a breathless peck on the cheek, then turned a brilliant smile toward me. "Doesn't Skylar look great?"

"You both do." But Chris's eyes never strayed from my sister.

"We need to go," Connor said, a hint of impatience in his voice. I tried to make eye contact, but he moved to the front door and held it open.

Chris and Abbie walked in front of us, snuggling together when the wind picked up, laughing about something.

I glanced at Connor, who still wore a stiff expression. "Nice night, huh?"

"I guess. If you don't mind cold weather."

I couldn't remember another time when he'd been so out of sorts. "Are you okay?"

"Fine." He opened the passenger door of his Tahoe like a secret service agent might for the president—face of stone and gaze beyond me.

I sank into the seat, fingers knotting as I fretted. Clearly, he was mad at me. What could I have possibly done? At school yesterday, everything had been fine. Great, even. We spent five minutes laughing so hard we couldn't talk. What changed between dropping him at his house yesterday and opening the door for him tonight?

When we entered the country club banquet room, Mom's face filled with relief. "There you are."

"This looks great," I said, and it really did. She'd draped the room in silver and navy blue, and all the fussy food with names I couldn't remember smelled incredible.

Abbie shrugged out of her coat. "How's everything going?"

"The idiot florist didn't bring near enough votives. I wanted the entire room bathed in candlelight, and there's no way that can happen now."

"Mom, relax." I touched her shoulder. "It's wonderful just how it is."

She surveyed the room with her critical designer's eye. "You think so?"

"I love it," I insisted.

She opened her mouth to respond, then caught sight of my father entering the room, rumpled from his day of flying. "Oh, Paul!" She pushed past us. "You're twenty minutes late."

"How am I late? No one is here yet." He kissed my forehead. "Happy birthday, angel. You look beautiful."

I'd barely managed to say, "Thanks, Daddy," when Mom started in on him again.

"You need to go home, change, and hurry back. Skylar's friends will be here in the next ten minutes and I don't want you looking like a hobo." She brushed lint off his suit jacket.

"Teri, I'm tired and smell like an airplane. I'd like to shower and shave before making an appearance."

"Take all the time you need," I broke in.

Dad smiled at me, his eye creases deeper than I remembered. "I'll be back as soon as I can." He glanced at my mother, then turned and headed out the door.

Mom followed him out to his car. We couldn't hear what she said, but her mouth never slowed, and Dad's expression grew rock hard. Abbie took Chris by the hand and led him away, leaving me and Grumpy to our own resources.

"So, I guess you're officially part of the family if my parents will argue in front of you." I forced myself to chuckle.

Connor glanced at me but never looked in my eyes. "D'you want something to drink?" Then he walked away before I eked out, "No thank you."

You're not supposed to get blown off at your own birthday party. You're just not. I decided to march over and demand an explanation for his mood, but Lisa arrived. She carried an enormous gift and gushed about how great I looked, so for now I let Connor off the hook.

"This place is fabulous!" Lisa shuffled toward the gift table in three-inch heels. Why do girls buy shoes they can't walk in?

"That's a huge box," I said, watching her ease it onto the table.

"Nothing else would do for my Skylar." She noticed my curls. "Your hair is beautiful!"

"Abbie did it," I said as Lisa removed her coat. "Wow, that's some dress."

"You like it?" She spun so I could see the whole thing. Not only did it look like she spray painted it on, but it was red. It screamed, "Notice me!"

Lisa spotted Connor. "Hi, Connor!"

I was about to warn her of his sour mood when he turned and smiled. "Hey, Lisa. Chocolate-covered strawberry?"

She helped herself to the food on his plate. "I saw you this morning on Santa Fe."

"Oh yeah?"

"You were in the car with your mom. I was at Swim Quik."

He popped a cheese cube in his mouth. "Why were you at Swim Quik this time of year?"

Okay, what was this? To Lisa he was chatty and smiley? To *Lisa*? Connor didn't even like Lisa.

"I'm going to Barbados over Christmas." She helped herself to another strawberry. Was she so lazy she couldn't fix her own plate? She had to steal Connor's food?

"I've never been to Barbados," Connor said. "I've been to St. Lucia."

"When did you go there?" I asked.

"Couple years ago." He didn't even glance at me.

"Did you like it?" I said as he asked Lisa, "Who are you going to Barbados with?"

Unbelievable. When I noticed Eli arriving, I didn't feel an ounce of guilt about abandoning Connor to Lisa's motoring mouth. Alexis and John showed up a few minutes later. Alexis instantly noticed Lisa and glared at her, but Lisa seemed incapable of seeing anything but Connor.

Jodi, who always enjoyed making an entrance, strutted through the door twenty minutes late on the dot. She wore her makeup too heavy and her hair stick straight. She announced her presence by crying, "Where's the birthday girl?" and giving me a lavish hug, all arms and no feeling. "Sorry I'm so late. Catch me up, girls. What's going on around here?"

Alexis obliged in her low, gossipmonger voice. "This is so weird." She pointed to Lisa and Connor standing at a cocktail round. "Lisa's been hanging all over him. What's going on with them?"

Jodi's eyes sparked with jealousy. "I don't know. Skylar?"

"Like I told Alexis—nothing," I said as Lisa's head fell back with laughter. She touched Connor on the arm, one of her favorite flirting moves. I narrowed my eyes. "I can't believe Connor would let her do that. Obviously, she's using him to make John jealous. Connor hates games."

Jodi swiped the maraschino cherry from Alexis's drink. "Maybe not when they involve girls who look as good as Lisa."

"Red is a lousy color on her," Alexis said.

Jodi responded with a hearty nod. "Absolutely. It washes her out."

"She could maybe get away with a deep red, like crimson."

"Or brick."

"But not bright red. On Oprah last week, they were doing makeovers and—"

That's when I heard it—Connor laughing.

I couldn't take it anymore. "I'm getting another Coke," I interrupted as I walked away.

An actual laugh from Connor was rare. He smiled constantly and chuckled when he found something amusing, but the only people who made him laugh were his brothers, his dad, and me. Now he dared to do it at *my* birthday party because of something *Lisa* said. Lisa! The girl wearing glitter eye shadow as if this was a game of dress up rather than my eighteenth birthday party.

I headed for them, determined to break up their conversation, though I had no idea how to achieve this. Halfway there, Eli stepped in my path. "Hey."

"Hey." Beyond him, Connor excused himself from Lisa and headed for the food table. Finally.

"Can I talk to you for a minute?" Eli pushed his hands deep into his pockets and rocked onto his heels.

With Connor nearby debating cookie options and Lisa wandering toward Jodi and Alexis, I could focus. "Sure. What's going on?"

"Nothing. I just haven't had much of a chance to talk to you tonight. How's your birthday been?"

"Fine." I took a sip of my Coke. "My dad was out of town most of today, and Mom was over here getting ready for the party, so Abbie and I just hung out."

"That sounds great."

I shrugged. "It was okay."

"You look beautiful, by the way."

I smiled and fiddled with an earring. "Thanks. You look nice too."

He didn't respond for a moment, just gave me that smile, the one that could confuse a girl's heart. "So, listen—"

"Picture!" Abbie interrupted. She waited a second before snapping the shot, then pranced off.

I blinked away the spots the flash left behind. "What were you saying?"

Eli shifted his weight from foot to foot. "Just that I've been thinking a lot about us recently."

I gripped my cup tighter. "Are you breaking up with me at my own party?"

He laughed. "Of course not. The opposite, really."

"What's the opposite? Asking me out again?"

Eli reached for my hand. "I think we should tell your mom about us. I think we should ask for permission to be a real couple."

I pulled my hand free and glanced at my mom. She fussed with votives at a table across the room. No way could she hear this conversation, but still I lowered my voice. "Eli, I can't do that. My mom would go crazy."

He leaned closer. "Isn't it worth the risk if we can be together? Skylar, I love you."

I needed to do something, say something. I couldn't just blink at him with my mouth hanging open every time he said he loved me.

Connor materialized at my side. He took hold of my arm. "Skylar, I need to talk to you."

I glanced at Eli, who looked as off-kilter as I felt. "I'll be right back."

Connor dragged me to a relatively private corner. "Whew, that was close, wasn't it?" He gave my back a friendly slap. "I could tell you had no idea what to do."

I took a deep, calculated breath. "What are you talking about?"

"Eli. I heard him saying all that stuff about telling your mom. That's just crazy. I mean, doesn't he realize your mom would *kill* you?" He stopped talking when he noticed I wasn't exactly thanking him. "You did want out of that conversation, didn't you?"

I crossed my arms. "As a matter of fact, no, I didn't."

"Skylar, the guy just blindsided you at your own birthday party."

"Well, at least *he's* talking to me."

His forehead creased. "Do you mean me?"

"Of course I mean you." I kept my voice as low as I could.

"You've hardly said a word to me all night. I thought you were in a lousy mood, but then I heard you laughing with Lisa. Laughing, Connor. Laughing."

"Why do you keep saying 'laughing'?"

I pressed my fingertips to my temples, hoping to relax my left eye before Connor noticed it twitching. "What do I have to do to get your attention?" I could feel the tears building. This was not good.

"Lisa and I were just talking."

"What about earlier when you blew me off? Did I do something? Are you angry?"

"Of course not," Connor said, his voice soft.

"Then why won't you talk to me? Why won't you even look at me? It's my birthday, Connor."

He hesitated. "Let's not talk about this right now, okay?"

"No." I grabbed his arms, desperate to keep him there with me. "Best friends talk to each other, and aren't we best friends?"

"*That's* my problem, Skylar," he snapped. "You're my best friend, but tonight you look so incredibly beautiful I can hardly function around you."

Two seconds ago, I wanted to hit him. Now I laughed, overjoyed.

Connor's cheeks burned crimson. "I know. I'm sorry."

"I'm not laughing at you." I pressed his hand between mine. "I'm just surprised. I've been hoping—"

The rising chorus of "Happy Birthday" floated across the room and drowned out my admission. Abbie walked toward us carrying a glowing ice cream cake. She grinned at me. "Make a wish."

I didn't need to. I'd just gotten what I wanted.

13

Connor and I had only a moment's privacy during the remainder of the night. He used it to say, "Wait to open my present until you're alone."

"Okay," I said, and that was it. We didn't even have time for a private good night. Several minutes after I opened gifts, I caught sight of his Tahoe pulling out of the parking lot.

I hunted down Abbie, who had gone to Mom's car for a box of trash bags. "Did Connor and Chris just leave?"

"Yeah. Pretty suddenly." She offered a careless shrug. "Who knows?"

I eagerly awaited the party's end so I could rip into Connor's gift. I stared at its generous size and fantasized about what the tidy wrapping job concealed. Of course, I knew I should ground my hopes. Gifts from guys often left something to be desired. Case in point, Eli gave me his old baseball jersey. He claimed he thought I'd like something "fun" to wear to his games, but clearly he meant it to brand me as his.

How had I ever thought I could make it work with him? Eli was a nice enough guy, and he'd been a great friend. For some other girl he'd be perfect, but he'd never be right for me. Of course, with two unreturned "I love yous," he likely understood that now. Maybe he too realized we weren't good for each other. Maybe things between us could go back to the way they were before that stupid party.

In the privacy of my room, as I ripped away the silver paper, I couldn't help thinking of that summer night when I'd first met Connor. He'd been so aggravating, the last guy I ever thought I'd fall for. And maybe that's how it happened. Because I never viewed him as a prospect, I didn't worry about keeping him at arm's length. I allowed him to see me—the real me, not just the Skylar I was in front of my friends—and because he accepted me despite my flaws, he'd proven himself worthy of my heart.

My breath caught when I tore away the paper. Connor hadn't disappointed. I ran my hand along the lid of the sewing box crafted with glossy maple wood. My name was stenciled on the lid, and the note inside read, "Something to help you make your crazy outfits."

It was perfect. Just like him.

My cell phone buzzed and I grinned at the sight of Connor's name. "Thanks for the sewing box," I answered his call. "It's beautiful."

"Oh, uh . . ." It appeared I'd thrown him off. "I'm glad you like it."

"I love it. So . . ." I couldn't stop smiling. "Quite a night."

"Can I come over?"

I looked at the clock. "It's kinda late—"

"This won't take long. I just . . . I need to see you."

I clutched a hand to my chest, afraid that otherwise my heart would burst right out. I'd never felt this way with Eli. "I guess I can sneak out."

"I'll be right over."

"Okay, well I'll—" I stopped talking when I realized he'd hung up.

I examined myself in the mirror. Of course my hair looked frightful since I'd just unpinned it from its elaborate style. I did my best to smooth it, then tugged on a stocking cap. After two coats of mascara and a dab of lip gloss, I crept downstairs and out the front door.

Connor stood on the sidewalk, blowing on his hands. He appeared to have walked.

"Thanks for doing this." He stuffed his hands into his coat pockets. "I know you could get in a lot of trouble."

The smile glued to my face all night widened. "I guess you're worth it."

"Look." He swallowed. "I think there's been a misunderstanding."

Just like that, my smile evaporated. "What do you mean?"

"I think you took something I said the wrong way."

My teeth ground together. "I know what it means to have a misunderstanding. I don't know what I misunderstood."

But that was a lie. I could see it on his face.

"When I said you were beautiful, I didn't mean . . ." Connor trailed off. I'd never seen him so uncomfortable.

"Just say it, Connor."

"I didn't mean I wanted to be your boyfriend."

I glared at him, but my cheeks still ached from smiling. How quickly things could change. "You said you were attracted to me. If you're attracted, why wouldn't you want to be my boyfriend?"

"It's complicated."

"No it isn't. If you like someone, you want to date them."

Connor held eye contact with me. "Not necessarily."

"You're just scared," I said. "You're afraid of ruining the friendship, but things will be even better. You'll see."

"I'm not scared."

"Then what's wrong?"

He looked around the dark neighborhood and lowered his voice, as if someone might be listening even this early in the morning. "Please don't make me say something that's just going to hurt you. Let's leave this alone, okay?"

I planted my hands on my hips. "You know that's never going to happen."

Connor paced the width of the sidewalk. "I'm such an idiot." He tugged at his hair. "Why did I tell you I think you're beautiful?"

"I already knew you thought that."

He didn't say anything, just continued pacing. I tried to be patient, but I had limits. "So . . . what now?"

He stopped moving, looked at me. "What do you mean?"

"I mean, what happens now?"

"We're friends. Best friends."

I clamped my teeth over my lower lip until I knew I could speak without crying. This was embarrassing enough without an emotional breakdown. "I don't understand. If you're attracted to me, then what's the problem? Is it my mom?"

"No."

"Jodi?"

"Of course not."

"Then what?"

Irritation seeped into his voice. "Stop pushing, okay?"

"I won't. I want you to tell me, honestly, why you won't date me."

Connor's hands raked through his hair over and over. Finally, he said, "As a favor to me, I'm begging you to not make me discuss this anymore."

"I'm a tough girl, I can take it." But Connor knew how soft I was inside.

He tapped his toe against the concrete several times and looked away from me. "You're just not my type."

"I'm not your type," I repeated slowly. "What makes me not your type?"

He shook his head. "I knew you wouldn't understand."

"Of course I don't understand." For a moment I watched him, so stiff and distant. "What about when you changed my tire?"

His eyes met mine. "What are you talking about?" But he knew.

"We had a moment."

"Maybe, but—"

"Maybe! You *know* it happened."

Connor took a deep breath. "Like I said, you're my friend. That's it."

"You're just scared—"

"No I'm not."

"You are. I just don't know what of. I know you like me. Everyone says you do, and I don't understand why you're resisting this so much, when—"

"Because I'm only attracted to your looks."

There. He'd said it. I'd begged him to tell me and now he had.

"Oh."

"After what happened with Jodi, I knew I never wanted to date someone just because she's attractive." Connor stayed perfectly still and calm, as if I were a wild animal that might turn on him with one wrong move. "I love being your friend, Skylar, and yes, you're one of the most beautiful girls I've ever seen. But I can't have you as my girlfriend."

I couldn't blink, breathe, or even think clearly. Two options lay before me—devastation or anger.

"Skylar, please say something." In the dark, he couldn't read my face and it had him nervous. I let him stay that way for a little bit. "Skylar," he said again. This time he reached for me, but I stepped back.

"No."

"I understand you're upset. I don't blame you. And I know this will probably change our friendship, but I didn't know what else to do."

"We aren't friends," I said, my voice low and venomous. "We never were."

"Don't do that."

I laughed. "When were we ever friends, Connor? You've made it very clear tonight that my only redeemable quality is my looks."

"That's *not* what I said." Connor sounded furious.

"Well, don't worry, Connor. I won't force you to spend any more time with my horrid personality."

I turned as sharply as I could in my pink fuzzy slippers and left him there on the sidewalk with his mouth hanging open, as if he wanted to say more.

I didn't cry until I got to my bed. The worst of it was that he hadn't even tried to stop me.

In my dream that night, Connor and I sat on the grassy hill at Sheridan's, like we had right after Fall Ball. He looked at me with tenderness and reached for my hand. Then his face filled with horror, and he scrambled away.

"Connor!" I called after him, but he kept going.

Confused, I opened my hand to see what had scared him. My palm bore a gaping hole into my body, into my soul. I ran my finger through it, pulling away cobwebs and a black ashy substance, as if I rotted away on the inside.

14

As if it wasn't bad enough that I couldn't get out of going to church and therefore seeing Connor, after the service Amy clapped her hands together and said, "You should all come over for lunch!"

I hoped Mom and Dad would decline. Instead, Mom replied with a warm, "Why, that sounds wonderful," and we loaded into the cars.

"You know, I really don't feel so good," I said as we drove. "Maybe you can just drop me off at home—"

Mom turned and gave me such a cross look that I didn't make another attempt to escape.

The Rosses' home smelled like fall, a warm mixture of firewood and the stew Amy had left to simmer while they were at church. Everyone crowded into the kitchen except me. I lagged in the living room, staring at my surroundings. That feeling came over me again, the same one I'd had the first time I entered the Rosses' house—this home was different than any other I'd spent time in. I hadn't been able to identify the fitting adjective, but now it involuntarily rolled off my tongue. "Authentic."

I glanced around. Had anybody heard me talking to myself? Just Cevin. He pressed his paws against my leg and offered a friendly bark, as if to confirm my conclusion.

How would it feel to be authentic? To be the same in the dark and the light, the same whether I was with my pastor or with Jodi. To be like Connor and the rest of his family, who weren't afraid of people coming close to them, because they hadn't built up an image to hide scared behind.

There was no question as to why I hadn't been able to recognize it my first time in this house. I hadn't known such authenticity existed. Not until Connor called me what I was and so desperately did not want to be—hungry to belong and fit in.

"Are you okay?"

I turned. Connor stood in the living room with me. Beyond him, the voices of our families blended into sweet background music. "I'm fine."

He stepped closer and pressed his fingertip between my eyebrows. "Your face is drawn right here. It gets like that when you're about to cry."

"Honestly, I'm not about to cry."

"You always say 'honestly' when you're lying."

I remembered then that I wasn't supposed to want him standing so close to me, that I'd decided to be mad rather than hurt. Wordless, I brushed past him and went to the dining room.

"Skylar, how do you like your American History class?" Brian asked as we ate. He and Amy believed in involving everyone in table conversations, especially Abbie and me. Normally I appreciated their efforts, but today I didn't feel chatty.

I shrugged. "It's fine. Better than taking any of the other history classes."

"Connor says your teacher can be challenging to work with."

I gave Connor a faux smile. "Connor and I often see situations differently."

Connor paused his eating to give me an exasperated look.

"What's your favorite subject?" Brian continued as if he didn't notice.

"I don't know." I turned my attention to stirring my soup. "I'm not really a great student."

Dad passed me the basket of cornbread. "They don't teach classes on makeup or accessorizing, huh?" He winked as if we'd just shared a bonding moment.

Amy, having a brain and therefore realizing this comment offended me, jumped in with, "I wish I had a fraction of your style and creativity, Skylar."

"We just bought her a sewing machine, and she's making a lot of her own clothes now," Mom said.

Amy's eyes widened. "How impressive."

There were five other kids at this table—couldn't they harass one of them? "I don't make a *lot* of my clothes."

"You made that skirt," Connor said.

I glowered at him. "Skirts are easy."

"I can't sew at all," Amy said with a laugh. "My mother tried teaching me thousands of times, but I never could get it. I'm too impatient."

Mom pressed her napkin to her mouth so as not to smudge her lipstick. "Skylar is completely self-taught."

Okay, enough about me. "Isn't Abbie's hair shiny?"

Amy gave a knowing smile, then indulged me by turning to Abbie. "You do have very shiny hair. Is it from a special conditioner?"

After dinner, I helped Amy with dishes. That's how badly I wanted to avoid Connor—I would rather do housework than be in the same room with him.

"So, you and Brian were high school sweethearts?" I asked as I dried Amy's well-used kitchenware.

"I met him first period of freshman year." Amy smiled into the soapy water. "I knew my life would never be the same."

"And you guys were together until you got married? You never took a break or anything?"

"We had our share of disagreements, but nothing worthy of calling it quits." Amy evaluated the pan she'd just rinsed and plunged it back into the water.

"I can't even imagine you guys fighting," I said. "You seem so perfect."

She frowned at my word choice. "Brian and I have our rough days—we're human—but we try to learn and improve from every argument." Amy examined the pan again. This time it passed inspection. "Every day in marriage, you either grow together or grow apart. There's no standing still."

I thought of my parents at the dinner table, two rocks sitting across from each other.

Amy noted my silence. "Why don't you go watch the movie with everyone else? You'll have plenty of years of drying dishes."

"I'm happy to help."

She raised an eyebrow. "It's nice for me when you and Connor fight."

I flushed. "Oh, that. It's nothing."

"I caught him sneaking back in the house last night. Or should I say this morning?" Amy returned her eyes to her task. "I'm aware it's more than nothing."

I didn't answer, just fell into my own thoughts.

Finally Amy unplugged the sink, signaling the end. "This will pass," she assured me, wiping food splatters from the counter. "You two need each other."

15

Sadly, I couldn't lift Connor out of my life like I wished. I avoided him with ease during the school days, only to find myself sitting alone in my car with him at the end of Wednesday. I glanced his direction and caught him zoning out.

I sighed. "Five more minutes, then I say we leave."

Connor shook his head.

"What?" I asked.

"You're so impatient. School has hardly been out ten minutes."

I leaned back and stared at the characterless building. "I like to spend as little time here as possible. Your brother is cutting into my 'me' time."

"My brother? What about *your* sister?"

I shook my head. "Abbie's finishing up some English project. Her friend Jenna is giving her a ride home."

"Has she told your parents yet?"

"About what?"

Connor gave me a look. "You know what."

The muscles of my jaw clenched. "I'm sorry. That's something I only discuss with friends."

Connor looked about to say something when Chris arrived, short of breath and red faced.

"What's wrong with you?" Connor asked as Chris climbed into the backseat. Chris responded with a glare and Connor didn't push.

Strange. Connor and Chris never fought.

On the road, Connor poked at my radio buttons, dissatisfied with everything. "Did you know we're having Thanksgiving together? Our moms arranged it on Sunday."

My grip on the wheel tightened. "Like it's not bad enough being your chauffeur. Now I have to spend holidays with you as well?"

Connor sighed and stopped trying to talk to me.

At home, I found Mom in the kitchen, standing in front of the open freezer. She closed the door with her foot because each of her hands contained a carton of ice cream. "Hi, Skylar, how was school?"

Usually when I came home, I found Mom napping or preoccupied with rearranging furniture. My school day and rumbling stomach never occupied her thoughts. "Fine," I said, trying to sound as casual as she did.

"Vanilla or chocolate?"

I placed two bowls on the counter. "A little of both."

She scooped from the chocolate. "Do you think black or stainless steel?"

"For what?"

"The new range and cooktop. I just can't decide." She pushed my bowl to me. "There you are."

I looked into the bowl. "Can I have a scoop of vanilla too?"

"Oh. Sure."

"Do we need a new range and cooktop?"

"I'm not going to pay all this money to redo the kitchen only to have an out-of-place appliance glaring at me."

I didn't say anything, just unloaded my backpack on the kitchen counter, where I normally studied. Eventually Mom sighed, as if no one understood her burdens, and carried her ice cream upstairs to eat before her afternoon nap. I ate mine slowly and stared at the pile of books I'd brought home. While none of my classes had formal midterm exams, most of my teachers scheduled a big test for the following week.

I'd barely cracked open my history book when the front door slammed shut, followed by Abbie shouting, "Skylar!"

I jumped at the sound and banged my knee against the counter. "Ouch!"

Abbie stomped into the kitchen. "What"—she threw her backpack to the floor—"is wrong with you?"

The pain in my knee vanished. "What are you talking about?"

"What possible reason could you have for telling Connor I'm pregnant?"

"I . . ." But I had nothing to say. She had me backed against a wall.

"That was not yours to tell." Abbie moved toward me and I scrambled off my seat, not sure how physical this might get. Abbie's temper had the nature of a tsunami—devastating large areas, indiscriminate of who felt the wrath.

I backed away from her. "I didn't mean to tell him. He overheard me. I made him swear he wouldn't say anything."

"Well, he told Chris," Abbie said as she closed in on me. "Did you notice how he's been avoiding me since Sunday? Finally today I'd had enough. I began pressing him. It turns out Connor had a little talk with his brother, letting him know I was in a 'delicate condition' and not the best girl to date."

"Shh," I warned. "Mom's upstairs."

"I don't care if Mom's upstairs!" She came at me with swinging arms, desperate to hurt me in any way she could. "How could you tell the Rosses? You think people like them, so perfect, so together, understand messes like you and me?"

"Abbie, stop." I grabbed her wrists and restrained her as long as I could, but one arm broke free and she knocked me in the jaw.

"You're so selfish," Abbie somehow screamed and sobbed at the same time. "All you ever think about are your needs. Did you tell him just to get closer? So he would comfort you? So he'd know you occasionally care about things other than eye shadow and miniskirts?"

"Calm down. You're not making any sense."

"Well, we can't all be as rational as you." Abbie spat out "rational" like a cuss word. "Some of us actually feel things for other people. We can't just bury our emotions."

I crushed her wrists with my hands. "Maybe I can be too rational, but at least I'm not running around getting pregnant."

A noise interrupted us. We looked to the doorway where Mom stood, her hair rumpled from sleep. "You're pregnant?" she whispered.

Abbie nodded.

Mom's face drained of color. She blinked rapidly, processing, and then she exploded.

Mom had many faults, but she'd never been a screamer. I froze as Mom yelled phrases like, "knew you were trouble," and, "grounded for life." Had she directed these comments at me, I'd have broken into tears and curled into a ball, but this was Abbie's language.

"Well, maybe I would have told you sooner if I thought you'd be the least bit understanding!"

"Understanding! My fifteen-year-old daughter gets pregnant and I'm supposed to be understanding? You're not supposed to be dating, let alone—"

"Are you aware of how stupid that rule is? All of my friends can date, and—"

"I made that rule for *your* safety so something like this wouldn't happen."

"You made that rule so you could control us."

"It really doesn't matter why I made the rule. The fact is that I'm your mother, and I can make any rule I want for any reason."

Abbie responded, but I couldn't hear what she said through the garage door as I fled the house.

Two minutes later, I turned onto the Rosses' street. Connor and Chris were outside playing basketball, apparently having patched things up. Connor stopped dribbling as I pulled into their driveway. Both of them stared as I parked. My car jutted halfway into the road, but I didn't care.

"Hey." Connor spun the ball on his index finger. "You come to play a little b-ball?"

I glared at him. "Chris, would you give me a moment alone with your moron brother?"

Smart enough to recognize the short amount of time between his conversation with Abbie and my appearing at his house, Chris turned a shade paler. He looked to Connor, who nodded and tossed him the basketball.

Even when Chris disappeared through the front door, Connor and I only stared at each other.

"Go ahead," he said, voice crisp. As if he had any right to be crisp with me.

"I don't even know where to begin."

"Then I'll start. I had to tell him. If you'd learned the same thing about Chris, wouldn't you have warned Abbie? Put yourself in my place."

I stomped my foot. "No, *you* put yourself in *my* place. It's bad enough I was forced to share it with you, but you said you wouldn't tell anyone."

"I know I did, but—"

"I said, 'Please don't tell anyone,' and you said, 'I won't.'"

"And believe me, Skylar, that was my intention—"

"Then I said, 'Even Jodi,' and you said, 'I promise.' I didn't know I needed to list everyone you're acquainted with and verify that they too were on that list."

Connor hesitated. "When I made that promise, I didn't know we were talking about a girl my brother would soon like."

"It doesn't matter. You promised!" Hot tears built behind my eyes. How could I explain this to him? He let me down. The one person I'd come to count on, the one person I could trust, and he'd let me down.

"Skylar." Connor's voice was soft, as if in pain on my behalf. "I didn't like telling Chris about Abbie. I didn't plan to, but after your party, he was talking about her in a way that . . . Well, I just couldn't handle him believing it could work."

"If Abbie wanted him to know, she would have told him. It wasn't your place to get involved."

Connor pushed a hand through his coarse hair and released a shaky breath. "Whether or not Abbie wanted him to know is irrelevant at this point. I hate to say that, but she's over three months pregnant, Skylar. She needs to tell your parents. She needs to go to the doctor—"

"That's not for you to decide!"

"It is when it involves my little brother."

I looked at him, stumped. Clearly, I couldn't change his feelings, and he couldn't change mine. "Fine." I fumbled for my car keys. "I can't force you to acknowledge that you broke a promise and in the process turned my sister against me."

"I'm sorry it has to be this way. I shouldn't have made a promise on so little information." Connor scuffed his shoe along the pavement. "That was my fault."

I yanked open the door to my car, irritated that I was angrier now than when I'd arrived. "But you're not sorry you told your brother?"

Connor shook his head. "I'd do it again."

How could I have ever thought I might be in love with him? "Do you remember what you said to me at Sheridan's? That I don't really like Eli, just the idea of him?"

Connor nodded.

"When you told me why you broke up with Jodi, I thought, 'This is a guy who's different, a guy I can respect.'" Tears blurred my vision. I didn't have much time before I collapsed. "I was wrong. I see now you're just like every other guy I've known. I loved the idea of you, but not who you really are."

Connor didn't answer. He just stood there and watched me back out of the driveway.

I didn't want to return home, I couldn't trust my girlfriends to keep quiet, and now that I'd learned Connor couldn't keep a secret, that left me Eli.

He answered the door with a confused look. "What are you doing here?"

I opened my mouth to explain but instead burst into tears.

"Skylar, what's wrong?" Eli opened his arms to me and I fell against him.

"I love you," I sobbed.

He'd kept my secret all these months, and he was here now when nobody else was. Did I need any more of a reason?

16

I didn't return home until a few hours later, when I could be sure the screaming had stopped. Still, I pressed my ear against the door before opening it.

"I'm home," I said to the eerie silence. "Hello? Abbie? Mom?"

No one answered. I paused there in the doorway, awaiting sound of any kind. I'd nearly given up when I heard shuffling upstairs.

I moved to the base of the staircase. "Hello?"

The sound stopped. "Skylar?" Mom answered.

I started up the stairs. "I don't know if you tried to call. I accidentally left my purse here. It's a good thing I didn't get pulled over, because—" As I stood in her doorway, whatever I'd been saying slipped from my memory. "What are you doing?"

She didn't look at me, just continued her task. "I don't expect you to understand."

"Understand what?" I tried to say, but the words caught in the lump in my throat. I swallowed and tried again. "Understand what?"

Mom ignored me and pushed a final stack of clothes

into her suitcase. The big one. The one she bought for two weeks in Europe with my aunt.

"Mom?"

"I can't do this anymore." She looked up, but instead of meeting my eyes, her gaze went beyond me, as if she was already gone. She zipped her suitcase and stood it upright.

"You can't do what anymore?" I asked as she wheeled it passed me. "What do you mean?"

"It means I need some time." She started down the stairs, the suitcase clunking behind her. "I've never been the type who had to be perfect at everything. I long ago resigned myself to being a lousy cook, a lousy mother—"

"You're not a lousy mother." But hadn't I been thinking the same thing only a few short weeks ago?

"I am," she said. "I never knew what to do with you girls. Paul kept saying lots of women weren't natural mothers, that I would grow into it, but that never happened. So I thought, 'Okay, I won't be a great mother, but I can at least keep them safe. Keep them from making the mistakes I made.' And it turns out I can't even manage that."

I trotted alongside her now that we'd reached the main floor. "Abbie getting pregnant is not your fault. If it's anybody's fault, it's mine. I'm the one who drove her to Lance's all those months. I knew what was going on, but still I did it."

Mom opened the garage door. "If you need me, call my cell."

"I need you," I said. She kept going. "Mom, I need you." I squawked it over and over, like a six-year-old. "I need you. I need you." But still she backed out of the driveway and left me there.

"Can I talk to Abbie?" I asked when Jenna answered her phone.

"She's not here."

I ran my free hand through my hair. I'd done that so many times in the last few hours, grease now slicked my hair. "I know she's there. Put her on the phone."

"Who's this? Skylar?"

"There's no use covering for her. I'll just come over."

"I'm serious, she isn't here."

I hesitated. "If you're lying to me, Jenna . . ."

"I'm not."

I chewed on my lower lip a moment. She sounded truthful. "Have you talked to her?"

"Not since I dropped her off," Jenna said. "What's this about?"

My throat ached from holding in emotion, and I could feel my left eye throbbing. I reached for Eli's hand and wove my fingers through his.

"Skylar?" Jenna asked.

I mustered up the strength to speak without crying. "If you talk to her, will you ask her to call me?"

"What's going on?"

I hung up.

Eli gazed at me. "No luck?"

I shook my head. "And that was my best guess too. Abbie always runs to Jenna's when she's in trouble."

He smoothed my hair. "We'll find her." He said it with such tenderness, I fell a bit harder for him. How had I not appreciated him all these months?

I leaned into his touch. “Thanks for being here.”

“Thanks for turning to me.” He cupped my cheek. “I thought . . . I don’t know. For a while now, I thought we were on the verge of breaking up.”

I offered an apologetic smile. “That’s because I’m an idiot.”

“You’ve had a lot going on.” He shrugged. “Apparently.”

His tone convicted me. “I should’ve told you. I just didn’t know how.”

Eli pulled away and tugged at the cuffs of his sweater. “But you knew how to tell Connor?”

“It wasn’t like that.” I reached for him and covered his hands with my own. “He overheard me asking Heather to pray about it. I never would’ve told him otherwise. If I was going to voluntarily tell anybody, I swear it would’ve been you.”

“Okay.” But he didn’t sound convinced.

“Please don’t be upset about it,” I pleaded, squeezing his hands.

“I don’t want to be. It’s just the thought of him comforting you all these months while I was ignorant . . .”

“Believe it or not, Connor’s not much of a comforter.”

Eli searched my face, as if he thought I might be lying.

“We never really talked about it.” This didn’t appear to satisfy him, so I added, “Most of the time, I couldn’t stand him.”

Now Eli relaxed. “I never understood what Jodi saw in that guy. He’s obnoxious.” He slid his fingers through mine. “Don’t you find him obnoxious?”

“He’s certainly not my favorite person today,” I said with a humorless laugh.

"Chris seems like a cool enough guy, but of course—"

I jumped to attention. "Maybe that's where she is!" I grabbed the phone and dialed. "Why didn't I think of that before?"

Eli watched my fingers fly. "You have their number memorized?"

Before I could defend this, Amy answered. "Hello?"

"Amy, hi, it's Skylar. Is Abbie there?"

There was a moment of silence. "She is. Would you like to speak with her?"

In the background, Abbie said, "Is that Skylar? I'm not talking to her."

"Tell her I just want to talk for one minute," I said.

"She just wants a minute," Amy relayed. Silence. She sighed. "I don't think now is a very good time, Skylar. Maybe later tonight."

My throat tightened once again. "No, I have to talk to her."

Amy spoke softly. "She just needs a little time, dear. I'll have her call you later." And then she hung up.

For a while, I held the phone to my ear and listened to the silence. Then I slammed it onto the table—the gorgeous black one that inspired Mom's redecorated kitchen. The casing for the batteries popped off and danced across the tile floor. Eli watched it, then turned his big, denim eyes to me.

"She won't talk to me," I said in an even voice.

"I gathered that."

"Our mom just walked out, and Abbie won't take a single minute to talk to me."

Eli reached for my hand, squeezed it. "She's just upset."

"Well, so am I. Is her anger more valid because she's dramatic about it?"

"Of course not."

"I should've had some breakdown on the phone with Amy," I grumbled. "Then maybe she would've sided with me."

"Of course she won't side with Abbie." Eli fussed with my long bangs, which draped into my eyes. "You think the Rosses would let some pregnant girl hang around? They're extremely religious."

"They're also extremely accepting. Knowing Amy, she'll take in Abbie as the daughter she never had. Abbie already has the name for it." Bitter tears stung my eyes. *I* wanted to be at the Rosses' right now, not stuck in my empty house with a shattered family to clean up. Why should this be my responsibility?

Eli's ringing cell phone interrupted my thoughts. He glanced at the screen. "It's my mom." He flipped it open. "Hey . . . Okay . . . Okay, bye." He closed it. "Mom says dinner is almost ready and you're welcome to join us."

I made myself smile. "That's really nice of her, but I'm going over to the Rosses' to make Abbie talk to me."

He stared at our joined hands for a moment, watching his own thumb caress the back of my hand. "Are you sure that's a good idea?"

I shrugged. "No. But she needs to know about Mom and she won't take my call."

"Maybe you could just tell Amy and have her tell Abbie."

"That's a rotten thing to do to Amy."

"I guess you're right." Eli drummed his fingertips on the table. "How about if I go with you?"

"You have to get home for dinner."

"You shouldn't have to go alone." Eli pressed my hand against his mouth. "We'll get through this together."

I looked at him, this great guy who wanted to take care of me. Waning sunlight came through the kitchen windows and lit his face, as if God himself had turned the spotlight on Eli. He was beautiful. How lucky for me that he'd stuck around through my months of pushing him away.

I leaned into him. "I love you."

He smiled and kissed me.

As I pulled into the Rosses' driveway, a sudden rush of nerves came over me. "Maybe you should just stay in the car."

Eli unbuckled his seat belt. "I'm here to support you."

Before I could respond, he stepped out of the Land Rover, ending the discussion.

My hand trembled as I pressed the doorbell. Which Abbie would I find inside? The scared, tearful girl who crawled into my bed when she first fell for Chris, or the feisty, angry one who came home this afternoon with swinging fists?

Connor cracked open the door. "Now isn't a good—" He noticed Eli and the corners of his mouth quirked. "Well, I didn't expect this."

Eli's arm pulled me even closer. "Why shouldn't you?"

"I need to speak with my sister," I said.

Connor averted his attention back to me. "Look, Skylar, we're all encouraging her to talk to you. She's just not ready right now."

"But she doesn't mind being around you? You're the one who told her boyfriend and started this whole mess!"

"I told her not to blame you—"

I snorted. "I'll bet you did."

"Do you think this is some conspiracy against you?"

"Don't talk to her like that," Eli said.

Connor looked at Eli. "She doesn't need you to protect her."

"Leave him alone," I said. Connor's face revealed his surprise. I shrugged. "At least *somebody* is supporting me."

Connor kept his voice low. "My being in here with Abbie doesn't mean I'm not supporting you. I didn't even know she was coming over. She just showed up crying and—"

I laughed. "Of course. Abbie cries, so she gets the sympathy. What about me? I'm the one who had to go home and find my mom packing her European luggage." I enjoyed Connor's shocked expression. "That's right. Apparently, my mom has decided she's done with the whole mom thing and is moving on with her life. And *that* is why I wanted to get ahold of Abbie, because I thought she might want to know. And I thought it would be best coming from me, but since everyone in your family is so intent on protecting her, *you* can break the bad news."

I stalked down the manicured walkway, my dry eyes burning. Eli remained at the door long enough to exchange a few words with Connor, then he was at my side.

"All I wanted to do was talk to my sister." My voice choked with tears that didn't fall. "Is that such a big thing to ask?"

Eli rubbed my shoulder. "He's being a jerk. He should've let you in. Believe me, when you walked away, I told him exactly how I felt about the way he acted—"

"Skylar!"

I turned and saw Cameron scampering down the driveway, his feet bare in the forty-degree weather. He thrust his arms around my waist. "Connor said I should hug you."

Warmth filled my heart as I squeezed Cameron back. I held him there for a minute. "You should get inside. Your feet are going to freeze and fall off."

Cameron giggled and frolicked back into the house, pausing to wave before he closed the door behind him.

When I got in the car, I saw Eli's eyes full of suspicion. "I thought you didn't like kids."

I smiled at the Rosses' front porch, where Cameron had waved. "That one's special."

Dad came home barely fifteen minutes after Eli dropped me off. It was the first time in two weeks that he might have made it home for dinner. Of course, that implied dinner was still an event worth being home for. Last week, Mom started serving us cereal and ice cream for dinner. Heating up frozen lasagna was now too much of a chore.

When Dad arrived, he came through the garage as usual. Looking at him, I realized it had been awhile since I'd paid much attention to his appearance. His handsome face showed evidence of late nights and his gray hair needed a trim. In the early days, before his company took off, Mom had cut his hair to save money. She'd drag one of the wooden chairs into the middle of the linoleum and drape a silly cape over his clothes. Mom didn't allow Abbie and me in the kitchen during haircuts—she didn't want us tracking hair all over the place—but we could hear them from the living room, laughing and chatting. I hadn't thought about those days in a long time.

"Skylar?"

I realized then that I'd been standing in the living room staring at Dad. I blinked away tears. "Hi."

He studied me a moment. "Is something wrong?"

I nodded.

Dad looked around the quiet, dark house, then he glanced at the garage door, as if realizing what was missing. "Where's your mother?"

"I have something to tell you about Abbie."

"Did your mother leave?"

I only blinked at him.

Dad took a few steps toward me. "Answer me, Skylar."

"I don't think she's coming back. Not for a while, anyway."

I expected to see Dad stunned. I thought he might curse and march to the phone and call Mom's cell over and over, begging her to come home, to talk to him. I did *not* expect him to place a large hand on my shoulder and say with confidence, "Don't worry. She always comes back."

"What do you mean?" I asked as Dad carried on with his routine—coat in the closet, keys on the hook.

"This isn't the first time she's left. Just the first time you've known about it."

I followed him into his office. "When did she leave before?"

"Hmm, when was the last time?" Dad set his briefcase on his desk and rubbed his chin with thought. "I guess it was the summer before last. She went back to Hawaii to stay with Grammy and Papa. That's where she usually goes." He smiled. He intended to lift my spirits, but this news only depressed me. "Sometimes your mom needs a break, Skylar, but she always comes back."

"Daddy." I looked at my shoes, embarrassed for him. "I think this time is different. She left because of us. Because of Abbie and me."

Dad frowned. "Mom loves you girls."

"She said she never wanted to be a mom."

He kept his eyes on his desk and seemed hesitant to respond. "You came along a little earlier than we planned, but we always loved you."

That triggered Mom's parting words: "Keep them from making the mistakes I made. And it turns out I can't even manage that."

"How early?" I asked.

"What?"

I gripped the back of Dad's receiving chair. "You said I came along earlier than planned. How early?"

Again, Dad seemed reluctant to respond. He rearranged a few items on his already tidy desktop. "I'm not sure I know what you're driving at."

"Abbie's pregnant."

Dad's eyes locked on mine as he sank into his desk chair. "Of course," he said, seemingly to himself. "That makes so much sense."

"When Mom found out, she and Abbie went at it. I left, and when I came home, Abbie was gone and Mom left a few minutes later."

Dad ran his hands through his shaggy hair. "Where's Abbie now?"

"The Rosses'."

"Good." He gazed into his blank desktop. "The father?"

"You don't know him. His name is Lance Hartfield. He goes to school with us."

"And he knows about the baby?"

I shrugged. "I don't think so."

"Well, we need to alert the father and figure out how to proceed. We might need a lawyer." His hand moved for the phone. "Do you have the Rosses' number? Let's see if Abbie is coming home anytime soon." When I didn't answer, Dad looked up at me. "Skylar?"

"You're making lists." Tears rolled down my cheeks, as if I needed to compensate for Dad's lack of emotion. "You haven't even talked to Abbie. Aren't you worried about her?"

Dad swallowed and dropped his gaze to his desk. "Of course." His voice was barely a whisper. "This is just what I do in a crisis, Skylar. I detach. I make lists. It's how I am."

My hands trembled as I planted them on my hips. "That's a fine way to handle business, Dad, but this is Abbie we're talking about."

He just sat there, eyes lowered, so I left him alone.

17

I couldn't tear my gaze from the Rosses' front door. "Come on, come on," I muttered.

I spent my morning agonizing about this, seeing Abbie for the first time since yesterday's fight. With each passing minute—six total—parked in the driveway, my nerves wound tighter.

Was it intentional, making me wait? Were they all inside at the breakfast table, scarfing down buttermilk pancakes and laughing about my rumbling stomach? Connor said this wasn't a conspiracy against me, but the longer I sat out there, the more it felt like one. It was possible, however, that my hunger made me paranoid. I last ate at lunch yesterday.

Paranoid or not, I'd waited way too long for them to grace me with their presence. I forced myself out into the bitter cold and marched to the front door.

Amy answered my knock. "Skylar! What are you doing here?"

Usually I kept my attitude tucked deep inside around Amy, but this was too much. "I take your boys to school. Remember?"

"Of course, I'm just confused. Connor drove Chris and Abbie this morning. I thought he talked to you."

"Well, he didn't." I planted my hands on my hips. "I've been sitting in your driveway the last seven and a half minutes waiting on them. I could have driven myself to and from school almost three times by now." This wasn't Amy's fault, of course, but I couldn't seem to keep the words inside. "Not that anybody cares how I spend my time. I could've skipped school altogether today and my parents wouldn't have noticed."

Amy's smile was sympathetic. "That's not true."

"It is. When I got up this morning, my dad had already left for work." I crossed my arms over my chest. "Do you know what it's like to have parents who don't care about you?"

"Your parents care, Skylar."

"No they don't." I glanced at my watch. "But Mr. Huntley does, and I'll be late for first period if I don't go now."

As I backed out of the driveway, Amy watched from the doorway despite the brisk wind. She raised her hand in a slight wave, and my spirits buoyed.

Even with running all the way to American History, the bell rang long before I arrived. I winced at the sound. It couldn't happen with a worse teacher.

Mr. Huntley pounced when I stepped inside the room. "Skylar, I need you in your seat when the bell rings. Consider this a warning. Next time I'll count you tardy."

Thanks, Mom and Dad.

As I slid into my seat, both Eli and Connor said, "Where were you?" They looked at each other—two animals battling for the top.

In a hushed voice, so as not to draw Mr. Huntley's attention, I answered Eli, "I've been sitting in the Rosses' driveway."

"Why?" they both asked.

Eli glared at Connor. "Would you stay out of this?"

Connor ignored him. "Abbie said you left a message on her cell saying you wouldn't be able to pick us up."

"Why would I have relied solely on Abbie to communicate that? She's not answering my calls. Why would I assume she'd listen to voice mail?"

And suddenly I realized my voice was no longer hushed. All eyes in the room rested on me, including Mr. Huntley's. He peered over his half-glasses, his forehead deeply wrinkled. "Is my teaching interfering with your social agenda, Skylar?"

My face burned. "I'm sorry."

"If you and Connor would like to chitchat, perhaps you should arrive early to school."

I ducked my head.

Now that he'd sufficiently embarrassed me, Mr. Huntley resumed his lecture. Minutes later, Connor slid his notebook onto my desk. *I'm sorry about this morning. Please don't be mad.* I ignored it at first, but then he nudged it closer. I fixed him with a glare that would wither anybody but the ever-resilient Connor and scribbled a profane response. He shook his head with frustration, tore the page from his notebook, and aimed for the trash can. That ended that.

Or so I thought.

"What's wrong with you?" Connor asked the moment the bell rang.

I didn't answer, just continued jamming supplies in my backpack.

"You can't freeze me out forever."

I threw my bag over my shoulder. "I guess we'll find out."

"Let me help you, Skylar. I—"

Eli stepped between us, blocking my view of Connor. "I think Skylar has made it pretty clear that she doesn't want to talk to you."

"Fine," Connor said. "But tell your girlfriend this morning wasn't my fault."

I sidestepped Eli. "Not your fault? You were stupid enough to believe her. I'm supposed to be your best friend—"

"You *are* my best friend."

"Not anymore I'm not."

I exited, and while both guys followed me, Connor stayed right on my heels. "It doesn't work like that. You don't get a say in whether or not you're my best friend."

I hated that he thought quicker than me, that he was so articulate. In lieu of being witty, I picked up the pace.

"So this is how it's going to be?" Connor said as we reached our lockers. My friends, who were at their lockers, turned big, curious eyes our direction. "You're going to push me away, hibernate in your room, and feel sorry for yourself?"

"You're making me sound pathetic."

He shook his head as if disgusted. "You're acting pathetic."

He turned to walk away, but Eli's infamous temper flared—he grabbed Connor by the collar of his shirt and yanked him back.

I reached for his arm. "Eli, stop!"

But Connor appeared calm, even slightly amused. "Let me go."

"Eli, let him go." I uncurled the fingers gripping the collar of Connor's polo. "I appreciate you sticking up for me, but let him walk away."

Eli momentarily tightened his hold. "I'll only tell you one more time. Leave her alone," he said before releasing him.

Connor held my gaze for a moment. He straightened his collar and walked away, his steps as jaunty as if the whole ugly scene had never happened.

The girls crowded around me, wanting to jabber about what they'd just witnessed, but Eli reached for my hand and pulled me away from my clucking friends. "Give her a little space." He led me toward the parking lot. "Let's get out of here."

"You sure I can't talk you into ice skating?" Eli asked as he directed his car down my street.

I'd been resting in the reclined passenger's chair. I opened my eyes and offered a sleepy smile. "I'm afraid lunch, two movies, and ice cream are all I have energy for today."

"You should come over for dinner."

"And tell my dad I'm having dinner with my boyfriend's family?"

Eli shrugged. "Tell him you're at Jodi's or something. You'll just be two houses down. You're hardly lying." He slowed as we reached my house. "Last chance."

"Thanks, but I really need to get inside." With the car parked, I leaned across the console and kissed him. "I really appreciated today. You saved me this morning."

He rested his forehead against mine. "No way am I letting someone talk to my girl that way."

"I didn't mean Connor. I meant afterward with our friends. There was no way I could have dealt with them."

"Yeah, about that." Eli tucked my overgrown bangs behind my ears. "When are you going to tell them what's going on? I'm sure they'd want to help."

I snorted. "And I'm sure they'd want to gossip about me behind my back."

The corners of his mouth twitched upward. "Maybe just Alexis and Lisa."

"They're the least of my concerns. Jodi's who I'm worried about."

He frowned. "Why Jodi?"

"Are you kidding?" I tilted my head, evaluating him. Didn't he know this? "She'd love to get revenge on me for dating you."

"That's crazy." Eli nearly laughed. "You're just being paranoid."

In a quiet and what I hoped was a non-accusatory voice, I said, "She's been flirting with you ever since we got together."

"That's just how Jodi is." He punctuated this with a shrug, as if even he doubted this explanation.

"She's hoping to catch you in a moment of weakness and break us up."

"We're just friends"—his voice emerged sharp—"same as you and Connor are just friends. *Best* friends, apparently."

I bit my lip. How had this turned into a fight? The last few hours had held more laughter and intimacy than the last four months combined. All day I'd kicked myself for holding Eli at arm's length these last years.

I measured my words with care. "I was just trying to say thank you. I didn't mean to start a fight."

"You didn't." His fingers combed through my loose hair before cupping my cheek. "I'm sorry. I didn't mean how that came out. It's just . . . Connor."

"Why does he bother you so much?"

Eli shook his head. "I just don't trust him. He seems too good to be true."

I looked at my lap, not wanting Eli to see how tears pricked my eyes. "Apparently he was."

"Hey." Eli tapped beneath my chin with a curled finger, encouraging me to look up. "You don't have to rely on him anymore, okay? You've got me now." He pressed his lips against mine for a soft, tender good-bye kiss. "I love you."

I smiled and slid my hand through his blond hair. "I love you too."

After one more kiss, I went inside.

The sound of Dad's voice surprised me. What was he doing home? But more importantly, had he seen me in the driveway with Eli?

My fears eased as I approached his office, where the windows faced the neighbor's house rather than the front yard.

"Thanks, Brian. Any time is fine." Dad saw me and beckoned me inside. "I sure appreciate it. Bye."

"Hi, Dad." I dropped into his rarely used receiving chair. "Why are you home so early?"

He fixed me with a stern look. "*You* ditched school."

I swallowed. "No I didn't. I—"

Dad poked the answering machine's play button. The

raspy voice of Shawnee Mission's secretary filled the room. "This message is for Paul or Teri Hoyt alerting you of Skylar's unexcused absence. If this is a mistake, please call the front office or send a note to school with your daughter. Thank you."

Dad cocked his head at me. "Where have you been?"

If he cared about what I did, maybe he should've been here this morning when I woke up.

"Why does it matter?"

"I'm your father and I want to know. That's why."

"I've just been out, okay?" I crossed my legs, as if completely comfortable. "I didn't feel like being at school, so I left."

"Were you with anyone?"

"No."

"Really?" Dad leaned forward and rested his chin on steepled fingers. "Not even your boyfriend, Eli?"

My surprise showed before I could conceal it.

His mouth pressed into a thin line. "That's what I thought."

"How do you know about Eli?"

"Brian Ross told me. Apparently, he and Connor tussled today. You can imagine my surprise, seeing as you're not supposed to have a boyfriend."

"I'm eighteen years old—"

"I don't care how old you are. You know the rules, Skylar." He shook his head. "It's no wonder Abbie thinks she can disobey and get away with it. Look at the example you've set for her."

Guilt pierced my heart. "Abbie got pregnant before I started dating Eli." It was lame and I knew it.

"Well, you're not dating him anymore."

I laughed, loud and humorless. "You seriously expect me to listen to you? This is about the longest conversation we've had since we moved into this house. You're always at work."

"I know it's hard to understand, but it's my job as a man to provide for my family."

"Brian somehow provides for his family *and* shows up for dinner."

Dad's eyes narrowed at this. "You're just like your mother, you know that?" The second slap in the face. "You don't mind my working hours when you're at the mall running up the credit cards, but the second I say something you don't like, you're throwing my late nights in my face. If you had any idea—"

"You know"—I pushed myself to my feet—"I think Mom and Abbie had the right idea." I grabbed the doorknob and let his office door close with a satisfying bang.

It wasn't until I marched into the garage, determined to fire up the ignition and squeal out of there, that I realized my car was still in the Shawnee Mission parking lot. Perfect. I groaned and turned to walk back in the house, but my eye caught Dad's Mercedes. Well, it's not like he was using it . . .

Of course, I didn't have many options of where to go. As I cruised down the Parkway, I called Mom. She'd said I could call if I needed her, and boy, did I. On my first few attempts, it rang several times before voice mail kicked in. By the fifth call, it stopped ringing and sent me straight to Mom's prerecorded message, like she'd turned it off.

I tried Abbie's cell as well, unsurprised when she didn't

answer, and then pointed Dad's car in the direction of Eli's. I couldn't spend the night at his place, but I could at least eat a good meal and hang out with someone who cared about me.

The Wellings lived directly off the Parkway in a bulky, historic house that screamed wealth. In my sporty Acura, their driveway hadn't felt so narrow, but it did in Dad's sedan. At any moment I expected to hear the tires crunching a perfectly pruned hedge.

Mrs. Welling opened the door with a smile. "How nice to see you, Skylar. Are you joining us for dinner?"

"I'm looking for Eli. Is he home yet?"

"No." Her forehead creased as she considered this. "His car pulled in, but then he walked down the street. I assume he's at Jodi's."

The hair on the back of my neck bristled. "Jodi's?"

"He's been there about five minutes. I'm sure he'll be home soon if you want to come in."

"Oh, um, I was actually headed to Jodi's and just thought I would stop by and say hey. I'll just catch him over there." I backed off the front steps. "Bye, Mrs. Welling."

My pace quickened with every step, though I couldn't say why I felt I needed to go over to Jodi's. Sometimes truth is so blatant, you know it in the marrow of your bones regardless of visual, tangible evidence. Not that I didn't already have plenty of that. Like earlier, when Eli snapped at me in the car for mentioning Jodi flirting with him. James's party, how they looked at each other. Eli's paranoia about Connor and me.

Alexis's words at Sheridan's returned to me: "An absurdly jealous partner is often a sign that *they* are cheating."

I knocked on Jodi's front door. It wasn't until Jodi's little brother opened it that I realized I was still knocking. "Where's your sister?"

He pointed upstairs.

I jogged to Jodi's room, slowing only when I saw the door slightly ajar.

"Look, you don't need to stay to ease a guilty conscience," she said as I tiptoed closer.

"I'm not leaving until you swear you won't tell Skylar what happened."

As Eli spoke, I discovered a tiny flame of hope had still burned in my heart. Poof. Gone.

"Skylar and I aren't particularly chatty these days," Jodi said.

"So, you won't tell her?"

A pause followed. I shifted closer to the door and discovered a view of Jodi's full-length mirror. In it I saw Eli standing in the middle of the room with only his back visible to me. Jodi sat on her desk, facing both him and the mirror.

"Has it ever occurred to you that Skylar might not be worth all this?" She smiled as she said it, the toothy, fake one. "Neither of you has seemed happy since you got together."

Eli shifted his weight. "You don't understand the situation."

"What's there to understand? Skylar treats you like dirt and you let her."

He answered her quietly, "She's had a rough couple months."

"Yeah, her life's *real* hard." Jodi crossed her arms over her chest. "I wish my biggest concern was figuring out which boy to make fall in love with me next." She huffed a sad little noise. "What is it with you guys? It's like she looks your direction and you lose all common sense."

Eli didn't say anything right away. He seemed to be looking at her, but I couldn't tell from my view. "Just please don't tell her about Fall Ball. I was upset. I thought we were about to break up—"

"Eli, I got it. I promise not to tell your precious girlfriend you turned to me in a moment of weakness."

I'd have marched in then and there, but I was too busy vibrating with anger.

"Thanks." But even with the promise secured, Eli didn't seem to be in a hurry to get out of there. "You know, Jodi, you're always going to be special to me. I'm always going to love you."

That did it.

I pushed open the door. "And here I thought I was the only one."

Eli yelped.

I glared at him. "Yeah, sorry, I guess I wasn't supposed to hear that, was I?"

He reddened but didn't speak. I cut my gaze to Jodi, who wore a satisfied expression—victory clearly belonged to her.

"You know, I planned to humiliate you publicly"—she tipped her head from side to side, as if weighing the pros and cons—"but this works well too."

I studied her. This tension between us had gone on for so long, I couldn't remember what we were like before. "I can't believe I ever considered you my best friend."

Jodi set her jaw. “Right back at you.”

“And you.” I turned to Eli. Clever remarks bounced around my brain, but when I saw him standing there, so sheepish and pathetic, it didn’t seem worth it.

So I just shook my head and left.

18

As if the day hadn't been long and trying enough, I came home to find Connor's Tahoe parked in the driveway and the owner himself standing in Abbie's bedroom.

"Nice to see you feel at home," I said.

Connor turned from Abbie's open dresser drawers, his smile sheepish. "Your dad let me in."

"Unbelievable."

"I was pretty shocked myself. I thought he'd either escort me upstairs and stand guard, or make me sit in the entryway until you got home."

"Normally he would. I guess he's a little distracted right now." I crossed my arms. "Why are you here, anyway?"

"Abbie needs clothes."

"And she doesn't have legs?"

"I volunteered to come over."

I didn't think I wanted to know, but I asked anyway. "Why?"

"I wanted to see you."

Yep, I'd been right. I didn't want to know.

I dropped onto Abbie's bed, a sleep-deprived ache building behind my eyes. "And it doesn't matter that I don't want to see you?"

"I wanted to apologize for this morning. I never should've said what I did. If you don't want to talk to me, that's your prerogative. From now on—" He squinted, examining me. "Have you been crying?"

I laughed humorlessly. "What happened to it being my prerogative?"

"Sorry, of course. If you don't want to talk, that's fine." He turned back to Abbie's drawers. "Mind doing me a favor?"

"What?"

"Can you pack for Abbie? I really don't want to rifle through her dresser."

"No way. If Abbie wants clothes, she can walk over here herself and get them."

Connor sighed. "Don't do it for Abbie, do it for me. Please."

"I guess I do owe you." I dragged myself off the bed. "After all, if it wasn't for you, my mom never would have left and Abbie wouldn't hate me."

Connor studied me, but I didn't look at him. "You know I never meant for this to happen."

I forced up the corners of my mouth. "Thanks. That fixes everything."

"Stop it," Connor snapped. "I can't take anymore of this surly, sarcastic Skylar. That's the girl I met this summer. That's not you."

"I *am* that girl."

"No you're not. I know better."

"You're wrong." I felt the evidence of it in my back pocket. "I was stupid to think I could change." I jammed wads of Abbie's pajamas into the duffle bag Connor held out. "You need new scenery to really change, like college. Nearly being raped just doesn't cut it."

I didn't realize the words escaped my mouth until Connor's fingers curled around my arm. "Eli?"

I sniffled, congested from all the crying I'd done while aimlessly driving around the city. "No."

"Then who?"

"No one you know." I pulled away from his touch and pushed a stack of Abbie's sweaters between us.

"Aaron?"

The sound of his name made me shiver. "Who told you about him?" It came out as a whisper.

Connor kept his voice quiet as well. "Jodi. She said you'd been hanging all over him one night, then suddenly you were with Eli and never even mentioned Aaron again."

My hands trembled as I turned to the closet and yanked clothes from hangers. I wasn't packing anymore, I was ripping Abbie's room apart—same as I wanted to do to my messy, chaotic life. "I don't like talking about him."

Connor stayed near the dresser. "Maybe you should."

I laughed. "Why does everyone say that? Talking about it isn't going to change what happened."

"Maybe it'll make you feel better."

"And maybe it won't."

"It doesn't look like you could feel much worse."

"Fine, you want to hear about it?" Abbie's clothes now covered the floor. I started on her shoes. "In July, Jodi's parents went away for their anniversary and she threw a party. I met Aaron there. He was a friend of a friend. A senior at one of the Blue Valley schools. I'd seen him at a couple parties before, but we'd never talked, and I liked him right away. He was funny, really cute—"

"Ouch!"

I turned and found I'd clocked him with Abbie's boot.

Connor rubbed his knee. "Could you maybe tell the story without throwing shoes?"

"Fine." I plopped on the floor and started folding pants. "I drank a lot that night. More than normal. I think I was trying to impress Aaron or something. I'd never really liked someone before and didn't know how to act."

I pressed my teeth into my lower lip to keep from crying.

Connor sat beside me. He picked up a shirt to fold. "You can cry if you want."

I stopped fussing with Abbie's clothes and stared into my lap. "I don't even remember going upstairs, but suddenly we were there. It was the guest bedroom, the one Jodi's mom didn't like us going into because she was just sure we would break or scratch something. I felt awful. Kind of nauseous and really thirsty. I told Aaron, but he wouldn't let me leave and I started to cry."

As if on cue, tears spilled down my cheeks, but I forced myself to keep going. "Eli heard me. He was jealous of Aaron and had been watching us all night. He said he saw Aaron put something in my drink and that's why he followed us upstairs." I shrugged. "I guess it's true. I don't really remember."

"And this is why you've stuck by Eli," Connor said. "Because he saved you."

"He got there before anything happened, but if he hadn't come along when he did . . ." I became too emotional to talk. Here I'd thought Eli was some kind of savior, but he wasn't. He was human. So was Connor. Wasn't there anyone in life who wouldn't let me down?

"I don't remember much else," I continued once I mastered my vocal cords. "I passed out not too long after Eli burst in the room. I woke up in his car, where apparently I'd slept off the roofy, or whatever it was Aaron gave me."

"How scary." Connor covered my hand with his. "I'm really sorry."

I didn't want his sympathy. I stood. "That'll last Abbie for a while. You should go home."

He stood along with me. "You *have* changed, you know. Whether you feel like it or not. You're not like your friends anymore."

I challenged him with my eyes. "Does dressing different make me different?"

His face took on an expression I'd never before seen. Embarrassment? "Don't do that. I didn't know you when I said that."

"Maybe you should have waited until you knew me to judge."

"You're not the easiest person to get to know." His embarrassment gave way to a smile. "It took me a long time to discover how special you are. How strong you are."

I laughed a nervous laugh. "Don't say that." My hand reached for my back pocket, to the lighter and pack of cigarettes I'd purchased on my way home. A little taste of my old life, of a simpler time.

"Why don't you and your dad come over tonight? I know my parents wouldn't mind, and Abbie would get over it."

I looked away from him. "Please stop trying to help me."

He stood there a moment, evaluating me. "Is this about your birthday?"

Heat rose to my face at the mention of it. "No."

"Because—"

"Look, I don't care about what you said. All I care about is being alone."

He sighed as he fit Abbie's duffle bag over his shoulder. "When you're ready, I'll be here." He kissed my cheek so quickly there was no time to react. "Good night."

I waited until I heard the Tahoe's ignition turn before I pulled out the cigarettes. Before, I'd been careful not to smoke even in my car, but now I lit up right there in Abbie's bedroom. I gagged at the smell of the cigarette smoldering and flushed it down the toilet. Watching it spiral around the bowl, I realized I'd ventured too far in this new life for the old one to be appealing. What a shame, because I wasn't sure I had the strength to get through the new one.

19

When I entered Shawnee Mission High the following morning, Lisa and Alexis's squabbling greeted me in the entryway.

Lisa stomped her foot like a spoiled three-year-old in Toys R Us. "Why did you even consider going out with him? He's my ex-boyfriend!"

Her screeching made my head pound. Why had they suddenly decided to have it out about this? I hoped they were too absorbed with each other to notice my passing.

"Please." Alexis folded her arms over her chest. "It's not like you guys were ever serious."

"We dated for a year!"

"Off and on. And off-and-on relationships are different than steady ones, so the rules are different about who can date him afterward."

A noise resembling a growl escaped Lisa's throat. "The rules aren't different."

Alexis lassoed me into the conversation. "Skylar, what do you think?"

I paused. "I don't really want to get involved. It's not my place."

"No, I'd like to hear your opinion." Lisa crossed her arms

as well. "You've been through a situation like this. I think you might have a thing or two to say about loyalty and regrets regarding hooking up with your friend's very serious ex-boyfriend."

"You think I'm not loyal?" Alexis's face burned red with the accusation. "What about you? You didn't even want him until he started liking me. If you could think about somebody other than yourself for two seconds—"

"Me? What about you? What about how I found out you were together? You haven't once considered how I feel about this—"

"Well, you haven't considered how *I* feel, so why should I—"

"John told me that he loved me, if that's not serious then—"

"You never appreciated him, and now—"

"And his mother adored me, so don't even think—"

"Loved that yellow shirt and you—"

"Stop!" I elbowed my way between them. "What is wrong with you two? John isn't worth it. Are either of you serious enough to date him in college?" Neither answered. "Then it isn't worth making yourselves miserable your last year of high school."

Alexis made a disgruntled *harrumph*.

Lisa planted her hands on her hips. "Then tell Alexis to stop seeing him."

"What! Tell Lisa to get over it and find someone new."

"Tell Alexis she shouldn't date ex-boyfriends."

Alexis's eyes narrowed. "Tell Lisa her shoes look like she bought them at Kmart."

Lisa gasped. "Tell Alexis she looks stupid with bangs!"

Maybe it was how low this fight had sunk, or how sleep had eluded me most of the night, but I couldn't handle this petty, selfish life for another second. "Enough!" They turned to me, wide-eyed. "You are two of the most self-absorbed people I've ever known."

"Skylar!" At some point Jodi had arrived. She looked at me with disbelief. "What's wrong with you?"

"What's wrong with all of you? You didn't think it was weird that I was just suddenly with Eli? That I started going to church? That I stopped partying?" I couldn't hold in the tears any longer. "We've been friends for the last three years, but none of you have noticed that I've been drowning ever since this summer."

Lisa's face broadcast her confusion. "But you still acted like one of us."

I looked at her through my sticky eyelashes. She was right, of course. I had wanted to change but didn't want to give up my life. And that's why it had been so hard.

"I can't keep this up anymore," I said, to both my friends and God. I marched right back out the entrance. "I need help."

I wound through the unfamiliar neighborhood full of mature trees and tiny Cape Cod cottages and couldn't help thinking this might be a big mistake. With everybody in my life letting me down, should I seek out one more person? Should I trust someone to actually care about and help me with my problems?

"Arriving at destination," said the soothing voice of my navigation system, and I turned into the cracked driveway of a small white house.

I should put my car in reverse, go home, and accept that people would disappoint me. My hand lingered on the gearshift, itching to pull it to "R." But Heather was inside waiting on me. She might even be watching now. So I set the parking brake and braved the whipping October wind.

Heather answered the door with a pleasant smile, but her eyes were puffy with exhaustion.

"I'm so sorry," I said. "I didn't know who else to call."

"Come on in." Heather stepped to the side and gestured for me to enter her cramped living room. "I made coffee. Do you drink coffee?"

"Yeah." Although the candy kind Starbucks made was the only coffee I drank.

I followed Heather through the living room into a galley kitchen. Everything was old and small—the oven looked like something suited for a girl's playhouse—but the cluttered space felt homey.

"Do you take anything in yours?" Heather asked as she filled two mugs.

"No."

She smiled. "My dad would like you. He's from Texas and thinks it's a sin to drink coffee any way but black." She nodded at the square table pushed into the corner. "Have a seat. Just shove that stuff out of the way."

I moved a stack of cookbooks from the chair and took a seat. My position afforded a view of the backyard, surprisingly large. "Your house is cute."

"Thanks. It's not much, but it's all mine." Heather set my coffee before me and settled into the other chair. "I couldn't handle still living at home in my late twenties. I had an apartment for a while, but I often have to sleep during the day and it just got too loud." She looked about her surroundings, face shining with pride. "I really like it here."

"So you're just getting home from work?"

Heather nodded.

Her kindness made me itch inside—I was undeserving. "Why'd you let me come over? This could have waited."

She shrugged and brought the steaming mug to her mouth. "You sounded serious on the phone. Plus, it was an easy night. Just a few babies."

"So that's what you do? Take care of newborns?"

Heather cocked her head. "Is this why you came over? To talk about my nursing career?"

I cupped my hands around the mug and stared into the black pool of coffee. "I don't know why I came over. There was nowhere else to go, I guess."

"You can't go home?"

"My dad might be there and we're fighting. He just found out I'm dating Eli Welling." I shifted in my creaky seat. "I'm not supposed to have a boyfriend."

"Ah." Heather leaned back in her chair. "How long have you and Eli been together?"

"Since July. But, actually, we just broke up yesterday." I swallowed and forced myself to say the shameful words. "He cheated on me."

"I'm sorry."

"You know, if it had happened a week ago, I would've been offended but wouldn't have really cared. But these last couple days, he's really been there for me. And now . . ." I tapped my nails against the blemished table. "He's just one more person who's let me down."

Heather nodded. "A sad reality, isn't it? People will always disappoint, whether they intend to or not."

"Really?" Tears stung my eyes. "I thought I'd come over here and you'd tell me that someday I'll find someone who won't."

She laughed. "I wish I could. Unfortunately, to err is human."

"So that's it?" I gripped my coffee cup with frustration. "I'm never going to be able to count on anybody 100 percent of the time?"

"No. Even that guy you'll meet someday who's going to love you more than anyone will occasionally disappoint you."

"So what do I do? Just accept that people suck?"

"Skylar." Heather leaned forward. "Why do you think we spend so much time at church talking about the infallibility of God?"

I shrugged.

"It's because there will be times in life when everyone around you is acting like the humans they are, and you need someone. God can be that someone. He *wants* to be that someone."

"I don't understand how. It's not like he can take me out for ice cream or anything."

Heather chuckled. "But what happens after your best friend takes you out for ice cream? You feel better for a little bit, but eventually the pain comes back. God is the only one who can heal the pain you're carrying around."

I raised the mug to my lips but couldn't force myself to take a drink. It smelled horrid. "But what if I'm in pain because of something I did that I knew was wrong? Shouldn't I have to learn a lesson?"

"Haven't you already? Isn't that why you gave youth group another shot this year?"

"But I only came that once."

"Why is that?" Heather asked. "What didn't we do for you?"

I plucked at the sleeve of my sweater. "It wasn't your fault. It just didn't . . . it didn't go the way I thought it would."

"Is it because of what happened with Connor?"

I blinked a couple times, trying to figure out what she meant. "You mean him overhearing about Abbie?"

Heather nodded and swallowed hard. "You have no idea how horrible I felt about that. I mean, I'm the one who took you in the offices. I should've checked to make sure we were alone. Did Connor ever say anything? Because I made it clear to him that what he heard was private."

It warmed me to think of Heather guarding my secret. "He never told anyone," I said. His telling Chris seemed way too complicated a story. And I didn't want to make her feel bad about something that so wasn't her fault.

"So, if it wasn't Connor, why didn't you come back?" Heather asked.

"I wanted to be a better person, and that stupid penguin softball game wasn't going to get me there."

I thought it might offend her, but instead, Heather laughed. "Maybe not you, but boy, every time I'm forced to play softball with a balloon between my knees, I'm reminded not to take myself too seriously." She paused for a drink. "Unfortunately, Skylar, there's no magic button you can push to turn into a better person. It takes a lot of time and help."

"How much time?" Once again, emotion threatened to overtake me. "Because I can see who I want to be, but I'm so, so far away."

"Who do you want to be?"

Like you, I wanted to say. I looked around the tiny house, crammed with old furniture and framed pictures. All those smiling faces frozen in time reminded me of the Rosses' house and their hung photographs. I guess there really weren't many moments in my life I wanted to capture and display for all to see. That was the difference between being cold and hard like me, and soft and sweet like Heather and Amy—they built a life worth remembering.

"I want to be nice," I said.

"Nice? You don't think you're nice?"

I smiled. "I *know* I'm not nice. I'd never take in some pregnant teenager. Or let somebody crash my place after I'd worked all night."

Heather thought about this a second. "So, you want to serve people?"

"But I don't *really* want to serve people. I wish I did, but I don't."

"That's completely normal," Heather said. "You don't think part of me would rather be curled up in bed than forcing myself awake with caffeine?"

"Really?"

"Sure. This isn't natural to me. I never would've done this a few years ago. I might have offered to meet you for coffee late in the afternoon after I'd slept, but never would I have done this." Heather leaned forward and rested her weight on her elbows. "That's the power that comes with allowing God to have control of your life. You're capable of so much more."

"But how do I start?" I asked. "Praying?"

"Praying is great. You can ask for a willing spirit and opportunities, but don't just sit around and wait to feel like serving because that's not going to happen. You have to just do it."

"I don't know if I know how."

"Sure you do. Just start with something small. You said you're fighting with your dad?" I nodded. "Do something nice for him."

"But I don't know what he needs."

"I bet if we give it a few minutes of thought, we can come up with something." She paused for a sip of coffee. "Tell me about your dad."

"He works a lot. He's always really stressed." Surely I could think of something nicer to say about him. Or at least something not so negative. "He drinks his coffee black too."

"There you go."

"What?"

"Make him coffee."

"I don't know how to make coffee."

"Then buy him coffee."

I resumed picking at my sweater. That sounded too simple. "But what's that going to do?"

Heather shrugged. "You'll have to try it and see."

"But I've never bought coffee before. Not real coffee, anyway. What if I order the wrong kind? Or buy it, take it home, and he's not there? Or what if—"

"Skylar," Heather said. "There will always be a million reasons not to reach out to someone. Sometimes you just have to suck it up and do it."

20

Mom's car sat in the driveway.

The smart thing would be to keep driving. This was between Mom and Dad, and I should give them privacy. I shouldn't stop . . .

I pulled alongside the curb and parked.

With a trembling hand, I carried Dad's coffee up the front lawn. I heard them yelling at each other long before I reached the porch.

"This is the problem I'm talking about," Mom said as I eased the front door open. "You want to boss me. You've always wanted to boss me."

They argued in the kitchen, allowing me to sneak to the top of the open staircase. I could hear perfectly without fearing discovery.

"I don't want to boss you."

"You made me drop out of school, made me stay home with Skylar—"

"I didn't make you do either of those things. I suggested you take time off once Skylar was born, but then you wanted to have another baby. I thought you liked being a stay-at-home mom."

"I assumed two would be easier than one. That they could entertain each other."

Dad laughed. "They're not puppies, Teri."

"You never encouraged me to go back to school. You liked having me at home."

Surprisingly, Mom was the one doing all the shouting. Dad kept his cool.

"Of course I liked having you at home."

"But you don't want me here now," Mom said, her words laced with anger. "You've made that *very* clear."

My body trembled. These last couple days, Dad had acted like he wanted Mom home. Why would he have told her differently?

"That's not what I said. I said you could only come home if things were different. If I stop working such long hours, you stop your excessive spending, and we return to counseling."

"Who put you in charge of this?" Mom snapped. "I own half this house and have just as much right to be here as you. Why do you think you can make demands of me?"

"Because I'm the one who stayed." Now Dad's voice boomed as well. "The person who leaves doesn't get to set the conditions for reentering the house."

I didn't hear anything for a bit, and then Dad said in a more collected voice, "I won't keep bribing you to stay with me, Teri. No more extravagant gifts, no more shopping sprees, and no more taking you at your word when you say you're ready to be a wife and mother again. We've done this for years, long enough that both of us know you don't need 'a breath of fresh air' or a few days at the spa to collect your thoughts. You need a life change. We both do.

"More than anything, I want you here with me and the girls. But not like things were. You can agree to come to counseling, where we'll start working to save this family, or you can walk back out that door. The choice is yours."

I held my breath, not wanting to miss a single word Mom said.

But she didn't say anything. Her footsteps echoed through the house as she walked down the hall and into the entry. Without breaking her stride, she took a wild swipe at the decorative vase sitting on an occasional table. I held my breath as it shattered against the white tile. The dancing bits of red glass so captivated me that I missed Mom's exit. The front door slamming startled me.

A ringing phone cut into the silence.

"Hello?" Dad said in a tired voice. "Yes it is."

This was perfect. I could pretend to be coming home just now and Dad would never have to know I'd heard his and Mom's fight.

I snuck back down the stairs, opened the front door, and closed it. "Hello?"

"I'm really sorry about this," Dad said to whoever had called. I walked into the kitchen and found him glaring at me. "I'll take care of it. Good-bye." He clicked the phone off and remained planted there.

"What's going on?" I asked in a too-chipper voice.

His hands shook. "That was your school calling me for the second day in a row, Skylar. Why aren't you there?"

"I . . ." But how could I explain to my dad that I'd finally cracked and yelled at all my friends before storming out?

Dad shook his head. "You know, it doesn't matter. Just get in your car and go back. I have enough problems without you failing senior year." He turned and walked through the kitchen to his office.

By the time I unstuck myself and followed, I found Dad typing an email.

"You should be halfway to school by now," he said without looking up.

"I know, I . . ." Dad's fingers kept tapping. I set the paper Starbucks cup on his desk. "I brought you coffee."

Now he looked at me. His eyes were the same dark cinnamon as my sister's, and I felt a sharp pain in my heart. I missed her.

His thick fingers curled around the cup. "Why did you do this?"

I shrugged. "I wanted to do something for you. They had two kinds, both named after cities or mountains or something. I just picked the one I could pronounce."

Dad continued to stare at the cup. I thought he would say something—at least "thank you"—but he didn't.

And then he cried. I'd never seen my father cry. I'd never seen him be much outside of irritated, stoic, or distracted.

"I lost your mother, kiddo." His tears turned to sobs. "I don't think she's coming back."

21

I rang the bell and hoped for Cameron. He seemed my best shot for making it beyond the threshold. Footsteps approached the door and I leaned closer. Not Cameron. These were too slow and loud. It could still be fine. So long as it wasn't—

"What are you doing here?" Connor asked, balancing on one foot. With the other, he kept Cevin blocked inside the house.

I set my jaw. "Look, I came to talk to my sister, and this time I won't just turn away because you don't think it's a good idea. What if it was Chris staying at our house and there was big stuff going on in *your* family? Wouldn't you want to talk to him? Wouldn't you be annoyed if—"

Connor pushed Cevin back and stepped to the side.

I marched past him. "Thank you."

Amy stood in the kitchen pouring a cup of hot tea. "Hi, Skylar. I didn't know you were coming over."

"Where's my sister?" I said.

She didn't bat an eye at my rudeness. "Upstairs. Connor can show you."

Connor matched me stride for stride as I forged the staircase. "I heard about you and Eli. I'm sorry."

"He doesn't matter," I said through gritted teeth. "Not anymore."

"Did something else happen?"

I landed on the top of the staircase. "Let's just say we need Abbie at home."

Connor pointed down the hall. "Chris's room is the second door."

Chris must have heard us coming because his gaze was already fixed on the doorway when I arrived. Abbie sat at his desk, her face turned toward her open textbook. Now that I stood there, I didn't know what to say. I hadn't thought this through.

"You can save whatever speech you have prepared," she said in a bored voice. "I'm not going home with you."

"You have to." I wanted to sound forceful, but instead, my voice dripped with desperation.

"I'm fine right here, thank you very much."

"You're being incredibly immature. Not to mention a huge imposition on the Ross family."

She glared at me. "They said it was fine if I stayed."

"That's because they're the nicest people in the world. That doesn't mean you should take advantage of them."

"Whatever." Abbie turned back to her homework.

"That's it?" I said. "You have nothing else to say for yourself?"

Her eyes shifted back to me. "The baby is fine, by the way, thanks for asking. Very healthy. The heartbeat is in the one-sixties. It's nice that you care."

The Rosses took her to the doctor? Jealousy pecked away at my heart. She was my sister, I was supposed to do those things!

"Abbie, you *know* I care about the baby, but you haven't wanted to talk about it. Remember all these months when I've been asking questions and you've shut me down?"

"I don't recall you asking about the baby. You wanted to know when I was going to tell Mom and Dad."

"A valid concern, by the way."

I glanced at our audience. Chris fiddled with a bit of loose string, appearing as uncomfortable with this confrontation as me. Connor offered me a slight smile.

"You know what you should've been concerned about?" Abbie turned in her chair to face me. "Did you know I need to be going to the doctor every month? That I need to be taking vitamins?"

"How would I know that? I've never had a baby."

"I could've hurt my baby, Skylar. Do you know how that feels?"

I sighed. This was a losing battle, a hopeless mission. I knew it when I left the house, but Dad had asked me to try. "Try and get her to come home," Dad said, his eyes still red from crying. "Tell her I'm not mad about the baby, that I just want her at home."

Fulfilling Dad's wishes seemed impossible.

"You should come home," I said, defeat lining my words. "Mom's gone. Dad really misses you."

Abbie snorted. "Dad doesn't even know me."

I clenched my fists. "Mom is gone—"

"You said that already."

"Dad doesn't think she's coming home, Abbie. Don't you care about that?"

She wasn't looking at me anymore. She said something, but it was too quiet for me to hear.

"What?"

"I said, it's not my fault."

I blinked at her. "Of course it's not your fault. Who said it was your fault?"

"Dad."

"When did you talk to Dad?"

"I didn't. He talked to Brian. He said it was probably good if I stayed here for now because Mom might come home sooner." She picked at a spot on her jeans.

"That's stupid."

Abbie shrugged. "Maybe not. She left because of me."

"She didn't. You can't blame yourself."

Abbie looked at me, the fight gone from her eyes. "At some point, you have to stop blaming everyone around you. You have to take responsibility."

"For yourself, yeah, but not for Mom."

Abbie sighed. "Just go away, okay?" She turned back to her homework. "I'm not ready to come home."

Frustration welled inside me. Didn't we just have a breakthrough? I thought at any moment she might jump up and pack. "Why is it up to you when you get to come home?"

"Why is it up to you?" she asked without looking up.

I stared at the back of her head for a moment, stuck.

Connor touched my arm, as if to say, "You tried your hardest. Let it be." I turned to him. He took my hand and led me away from Abbie. Mechanically, I followed him down the hall and stairs. When we reached the last step, I sat. Connor did as well.

"Why won't she let me help her?" My voice emerged as barely a whisper.

He pulled me against him. "I don't know."

"I care about the baby, I just didn't know to ask."

"I know."

"I should've just told Mom and Dad." I clenched my fists, driving my nails into the flesh of my palms. "They would've known about the vitamins and the doctor and stuff." I looked at him. "We could have hurt the baby, Connor."

"But you didn't. The baby's fine."

"No thanks to me."

"Hey." Connor coaxed my head toward him. He waited for me to make eye contact. "The baby's fine. Abbie's fine. She put you in a tough position and you had no way of knowing what was right."

"Maybe if I'd given it a few minutes of thought, but I was too busy thinking about myself." I envisioned my mom sitting on the couch reading decorator magazines while her two daughters snuck around with boys. She hadn't seen because she didn't want to. Just like I hadn't pushed Abbie to tell Mom and Dad because I was too apprehensive about the aftermath.

Dad was right, I was just like her.

"I can't do it." I curled my head between my legs. "I can't get my family through this."

"You can." Connor rubbed my shoulder like a trainer does a boxer headed into the ring. "You're an incredibly stubborn person, Skylar. You can do anything you put your mind to."

I uncurled and looked at him. "You really think so?"

He nodded and pushed his fingers through my hair, sweeping it from my face. "I do." Our eyes locked and his hand paused on the back of my neck.

"I should go," I said.

He nodded in agreement, but neither of us budged.

And then I was kissing him.

Who leaned first, how we forged the space between us, I have no idea. As soon as I realized what was happening, I yanked free.

"I'm sorry," we both said, scrambling away from each other.

I burst out of the Rosses' house and didn't allow myself the luxury of slowing down until I steered my car out of the driveway and onto the road. Then I took several deep, calming breaths and tried not to think about how much I liked him, how much I wanted him to like me, and how badly I wished I wasn't my mother's daughter. With my genetic makeup, how could I ever make a relationship last?

22

My hands quivered as I set my tray at a vacant table for four. I popped open my bottled water. Could I really do this? How did one go about eating alone? Where should I look? Looking down at my food seemed to imply shame. Looking around might imply desperation for someone to join me.

I solved the problem by eating as fast as I could while perusing my English textbook. Tears stung my eyes. Were people staring? Whispering about what a big loser I'd become? I didn't want to care. I wanted to throw back my shoulders and pretend to be the confident Skylar Lynn Hoyt I'd allowed everyone to see all these years.

What a relief to hear the bell ring. Such a relief that I forgot to avoid my locker.

The day of senior registration, when we all chose lockers next to each other, it never occurred to me that Eli, John, Connor, Jodi, Alexis, and Lisa might become the very six people I wished most to avoid.

Three of them—Jodi, Alexis, and John—already stood there when I arrived. I considered turning around, but of course they'd seen me. Avoiding them now would only make me look weak and ashamed, two things I wasn't. Or at least two things I didn't want them to know I was.

They stopped chatting and watched me spin in my combination.

"Where'd you get that skirt?" Jodi asked. I had my back to her and didn't realize she'd spoken to me until she said, "Skylar."

I turned. Lisa and Eli now stood at their lockers as well.

"I asked where you got your skirt," Jodi said.

I looked down. I wore knee-high boots with a striped skirt that reached my calves. "I made it."

Jodi's mouth quirked into a half smile. "That's what it looks like."

Alexis giggled. "Really, Skylar. Doesn't your dad make, like, seven figures?"

"But it's not as bad as that ultra mini she has. The mint green one?" Jodi pantomimed gagging.

Tears burned my eyes. No one had ever poked fun at my clothes.

"Guys, come on," Eli said, but quietly. Way to be a man.

"Or remember those barrettes last week?" Alexis laughed. "Those were so cool. When we were six."

I turned away, not wanting them to see me cry. My shoulder smacked into Connor's as I left our row.

"Are you okay?" he asked. I watched him note all my tells—the crease in the bridge of my nose, the twitching left eye. His fingers curled around my elbow. "What's wrong?"

A barrage of responses bounced around my brain. My

mother's leaving made me feel more like a child than I ever had. It mortified me that Eli cheated on me. I was dealing with things I never had before, like eating alone and mean, beautiful girls picking on me.

But mostly, I thought it'd be easy to get my life back on the right track, and now I realized it wasn't as simple as showing up to church. God and his plan for my life required me to do more. I didn't have the strength to follow through.

"I'm failing," I said to Connor.

"No you're not."

But he didn't know what I did, that if I could snap my fingers and return to who I was before the summer—the untouchable queen of the cool kids—I would.

A few days later, as I cut through the junior hallway to get to the parking lot and escape high school for the weekend, I overheard a girl I didn't recognize say to another girl I didn't recognize, "Abbie Hoyt? She's the sophomore with the really long, pretty red hair."

"Okay . . ." But clearly she remained unsure who they spoke of.

"Well, anyway, she's pregnant—"

"No!"

"Yes." With her long, straight hair and blunt bangs, she resembled gossipy Alexis. "Marie said she's actually moved in with the father."

"Who's the father?"

"Some new kid. Chris something. He's a sophomore too." She shrugged, as if this made him insignificant.

"I'm still not sure I know who Abbie is."

"Remember our film class? Abbie's the one who—"

"Whose sister is walking right behind you," I said.

Both girls stopped walking and stared at me. The girl with all the information stammered, "Oh. Hi."

"Oh, hi," I mimicked. "Who do you two think you are, talking about my sister that way? And who did you hear all that from?"

"Marie." Both she and her friend looked like they might pee their out-of-style-last-year pants.

"Marie who?"

"Marie Green."

"And who did Marie hear it from?"

"She said she heard it at her boyfriend's house."

"Who's her boyfriend?"

"Terrence St. James."

Alexis's brother. Of course.

"Stop talking about my sister," I said, then turned on my heel to return to the senior lockers. There I assumed I'd find the whole gang exactly as I'd left them—debating whose cars to drive to the night's kegger. Since all I wore today was dark rinse jeans and a black sweater, I hadn't given them much fodder for their usual conversation.

Lisa had just suggested her Jeep and Eli's Land Rover when I barged in.

"What's wrong with you?" I asked, my eyes locked on Eli.

He shifted his weight. "What do you mean?"

"I suppose I *should* clarify, shouldn't I? I could be speaking of so many things." Everyone in the hall stared at us, including Connor, who was in the midst of loading his backpack. "It was told to you in confidence when I didn't have anyone else to turn to. I didn't expect to be walking down the junior hallway and hear two random girls discussing my sister." Eli stepped backward as I came closer. "*Marie* told them. Do you know who Marie is?"

Eli shook his head. His back pressed flat against the lockers.

"Marie is dating Alexis's little brother. I assume you told John and—"

"I only told Jodi." Eli held up his hands in surrender. "I only told Jodi."

"Which is worse!"

His gaze darted between Jodi and me. "She said she was worried about you. I didn't want her thinking something was wrong with *you*—"

"So you told her about my sister?" I pushed him into the locker. Eli winced. "I would have rather you told her about Aaron than Abbie!"

"I'm sorry," he stuttered.

"I made a lot of mistakes this year," I said with an accusatory finger in his face, "but you were by far the biggest."

When I turned to leave, I found Abbie standing there, blinking at me. I couldn't read her expression and it made me nervous. Was she about to yell? I didn't have the strength for another fight with her, particularly in front of my friends. Or whatever these people were to me now.

"I'm sorry," I said. "You deserve to be angry with me."

She cast her gaze downward, and I walked away.

Starting my car, I spotted Abbie running across the parking lot. She opened the passenger door and hesitated. "Mind taking me home?"

At first, I could only stare. As we stood there, her secret raced around campus and I was the reason. This didn't make her angry?

"Hop in," I said.

She buckled her seat belt and swept her hair over one shoulder. She noticed my staring and shrugged. "Like it wasn't going to get around soon enough anyway." Then she inhaled deeply and wrinkled her nose. "Have you been smoking again?"

I was sitting at the kitchen table with Dad and Abbie, discussing plans for the baby over plates of fried chicken, when Jodi called. Staring at the screen of my cell phone, I couldn't remember the last time I saw her number flashing.

"I need to take this," I said as Dad detailed father's rights to Abbie. I backed away from the table. "Hey."

"Skylar?" Jodi said. "Can you talk right now?"

"I picked up, didn't I?"

"Look." Jodi matched me snotty tone for snotty tone. "I'm calling to apologize, so you don't need to be like that, okay?"

"What exactly are you calling to apologize for?" I asked. "Seducing my boyfriend and intending to humiliate me with it? Turning our friends against me?"

"About Abbie," Jodi interrupted before I could go any further. "I like your sister, okay? I never meant for it to get out. About her being pregnant, I mean."

"Well, good call on telling Alexis then. Really. A fabulous idea."

"It happened in a moment of weakness, okay?" I heard her grit her teeth. "Eli had just gone on and on about how he'd made a mistake, how he wasn't sure he could live without you. I wanted to hurt you back."

"I never intended to hurt you."

Jodi didn't say anything for a moment. Then in a quiet, vulnerable voice, she said, "That doesn't change that you did," and the line went dead.

Nothing short of Abbie's exhausted face and weak, "Would you mind terribly going and getting my stuff?" could coerce me into knocking on the Rosses' door at nine that night. As I stood on their front porch waiting, Heather's words danced around my brain, that I couldn't wait around until I felt like serving, I just had to do it.

I sighed as a stampede of little feet closed in on the door. It'd be so much easier if God would just snap his fingers and make me a better person.

Amy answered the door with Cameron and Curtis close behind, adorable in thermal pajamas and wet hair.

"Come on in," Amy said over Cevin's elated yips. "Abbie just called to say you'd be over."

I rubbed the soles of my shoes on the welcome mat before stepping inside. "Sorry it's so late."

"I'm just pleased you girls have worked things out."

Cameron grabbed my hand and pulled me inside. "We went to the pumpkin patch tonight. Come see!"

"Boys, you can show Skylar, but then it's bedtime," Amy called after us.

Brian and Connor sat in the living room, watching something sportsy on TV. I turned on a nice smile for Brian's sake. "Hi."

"Guys, give her some breathing room," Brian said to Cameron and Curtis. He rolled his eyes but wore a kind smile. Connor just blinked at me, like I was from another planet or something.

"Chris is upstairs gathering Abbie's things," Amy said after I'd properly admired Cameron's and Curtis's chosen pumpkins. "You're welcome to go on up."

"Great, thanks." I glanced at Connor, who still looked at me like I was a strange animal, then headed upstairs.

I found Chris zipping Abbie's bag. "I think I got everything, but probably not," he said without looking up.

I leaned against the door frame. "Thanks for taking care of her."

He shrugged.

"I'm glad she has you," I added.

He only nodded and stared at her closed bag. It looked like he might have recently cried.

"What do you think will happen now?" he asked, nearly whispering. "With Abbie and the baby. Do you think she'll get back together with Lance?"

"No," I said. "My sister is crazy for you, Chris. She never felt this way about Lance."

"But that doesn't change that they have a child together. Or they will."

"No, it doesn't," I said.

Chris continued staring at Abbie's bag.

"No one expects you to help care for this baby, Chris," I said. "But if you're going to end things with her, please do it now."

For the first time since I arrived, Chris looked at me. "She didn't tell you?"

"Tell me what?"

"She broke up with me this morning."

"But that doesn't make any sense."

Chris shrugged.

"What did she say?"

"That it wouldn't work out. That we're better as friends." He picked at Abbie's monogrammed initials. "Other similar vague statements."

"Chris . . ." But I didn't know what I could offer to make him feel better. Not when I agreed with Abbie.

He handed me her bag.

"Thanks," I said, and because it seemed there was nothing else to say, I left him alone.

I paused in the Rosses' living room on my way out. "Thanks for everything, you guys."

"Our pleasure," Brian said.

My gaze rested on Connor. He blinked a couple times.

"Well, see you all Sunday morning," I said, and headed for the front door.

Connor caught up with me in the entry. "Skylar, wait up." He stopped a few feet away but didn't say anything.

Abbie's bag was too heavy for me to stand there and have a staring contest. "What?"

"I . . ." He shifted his weight to the other foot. "You're dressing different."

I bristled. "So?"

"So . . . So, I miss your old clothes."

"Didn't you once accuse me of placing too much importance on my clothes? I'd think you'd be thrilled."

Connor shrugged. "Maybe I don't like your reason."

"What reason?"

"The girls making fun of you."

Had my skin not been so dark, Connor could've seen the blood rush to my face. "Well, thanks for sticking up for me."

He rolled his eyes. "You want me to be like Eli? Swooping in every time someone even looks at you wrong?"

"I'd prefer something between Eli's swooping and your idle standing." I fixed him with a hard look. "I need to go. Do you have anything else to say, or did you just want to add yourself to the mix of people critiquing my wardrobe?"

Connor opened his mouth, then closed it. He ran a hand through his hair, which desperately needed a trim. "I guess that's it."

"Great. Thanks for making sure I didn't get through the door without hearing that."

I charged into the frosty evening, the cold air refreshing my skin. What was wrong with him? Like I really needed more badgering with everything else I had going on. He wasn't supposed to be criticizing me right now—he was supposed to be helping!

Not that I'd given him much of a chance, I admitted, with all my mixed signals. First I said to leave me alone, then I kissed him, and then I pushed him away when he asked what was wrong.

Just like my mom. She wanted Dad to work less, but she still wanted freedom to buy whatever whenever. She wanted to be accepted back home, but she didn't want to accept the responsibilities of being a wife and a mother.

As I backed down the Rosses' long driveway and watched

the bare shrubs and solar lanterns pass by, I thought how nice it would be if I could do the same thing in life—if I could put my life in reverse and erase my mistakes this summer. Of course, I'd also want to erase prom night with that loser senior. And I'd gotten drunk after the Valentine's dance and said some stuff I didn't mean. I'd like to rid my life of those moments too.

And therein lay the problem. If I could go back and fix mistakes, how far should I go? The spot where I'd veered off the ideal path was fuzzy.

"God, please make the right choices obvious," I whispered as I backed into the street. "I'm no good at doing this by myself."

When I averted my eyes to the gearshift and switched into first gear, a thud sounded against the hood. I screamed and released the clutch, killing the engine.

When I saw what I'd "hit," I lowered my window and said, "Connor, what's wrong with you? You just took ten years off my life."

He moved to my window, his fingers curling into the interior. When he opened his mouth, no sound came out.

"What?" I said. "I'm in the middle of the road here."

He remained silent.

"Okay, Connor." I restarted my car. "I need to get home, so call me if you think of what you want to say."

"Wait," he said as I shifted into first. And then he kissed me. Or I guess you could call it a kiss. It felt more akin to him mashing his elbow against my mouth.

He pulled back, his breathing labored. "I love you."

Again my foot slipped off the clutch.

"Sorry." Connor ran trembling fingers through his hair.

"I didn't mean to do it like that. I meant to ease you into it, but then I just couldn't think of what to say."

He crouched beside the car. "Listen, Skylar. When I said what I did on your birthday, I really believed it. It wasn't until you showed up at my door with Eli that I realized how much I really do love you. And this last week, it just killed me when you wouldn't let me help." He sucked in a breath and met my eyes. "What I'm trying to say is this—I want to be more than your best friend. I know you're going through a lot right now, so we don't have to make any big changes, but I needed to tell you how I feel."

My body shook from restraining tears. "No." It came out as a whisper.

He blinked at me. "Did you say no?"

I nodded and turned away. "I'm sorry."

"Is this some kind of payback?"

"Of course not." I traced the pattern of my steering wheel. "You're my best friend, Connor. I couldn't stand to lose you."

"Who said anything about losing me?" He gripped my hands. "I understand you being leery, with what you're watching your parents go through, but—"

"It's not that," I said, withdrawing from his touch. "I just don't think it's a good idea."

"But why?"

"I just don't." I restarted my car. "I'm sorry."

"Skylar, no," Connor reached for the steering wheel and held it in place. "This is crazy. I want to hear a solid reason."

I glanced at my rearview mirror, where dots of headlights grew larger. "Someone's coming."

“Then tell me quickly.”

“Think about everything that happened with me and Eli.” I looked into his eyes, hoping I could force this to stick with him. “I’m incapable of having a serious relationship.”

“That’s what you’re concerned about?” Connor laughed as if this were ludicrous. “I’m not Eli. I know you. I love you.”

I bit my lip for a moment. “Look at my mom.”

“You aren’t your mom.” He said each word slowly. “If you hear only one thing I say tonight, I want it to be that—you’re not her.”

I thought of our left eyes, the way they gave us away to anyone who knew to look, and gripped the steering wheel. “She’s in me.”

“But she’s not all of you.”

The car behind me honked. “I’m sorry.” As I pulled away, I glanced at him, at his hurt and confused face. Better to hurt and confuse him now than trample him somewhere down the road like I surely would. Like Mom had with Dad.

23

Ah, Saturday.

Never had it been such a welcome day to me. Today there'd be no Eli, no Jodi, and most importantly, no Connor. Sure, Monday would be awkward, but Monday was two whole days away.

I stretched in the warmth of the late morning sun. I'd lain awake for hours last night thinking about Connor, about his expression as I drove away. Had I made the right choice? When a guy as wonderful as Connor wants to be with you, is it ever right to reject him?

No, no, no, I was *not* going to let myself do this. I wasn't going to ruin my entire weekend by dwelling on Connor.

With that resolution, I pushed myself out of bed and trotted downstairs for a late breakfast. No surprise, I found Abbie still in her pajamas. She sat at the kitchen table, evidence of a healthy breakfast pushed to the side while she studied a thick book.

"Good morning, Sleeping Beauty," she said without looking up. "I can't remember the last time I beat you out of bed."

"Well, don't get used to it. This was a special occasion."

I reached into the refrigerator for the orange juice. "I had trouble falling asleep."

Now Abbie looked up. "Something wrong?"

I pushed away the image of Connor's beautiful, hurt eyes. "Nope." I attempted pouring myself a glass of juice, but the carton's contents barely covered the bottom of my glass. "Abbie! You took the last of the juice."

"Don't blame me." Abbie patted the barely-there bulge of her stomach. She'd claimed last night that she was showing, but Dad and I disagreed. "Blame the peanut. I'm craving oranges."

"Well, what am I supposed to drink with breakfast?" I grumbled, staring into the barren fridge. "Mountain Dew?"

"Dad left coffee in the pot." Abbie gave me a faux-sweet smile. "You're welcome to it."

I made a face and filled a glass with water. I noticed Dad's empty office. "Where is Dad? Did he go in today?"

Abbie turned a page of her book. "He's at the grocery store."

"Those are words I never thought I'd hear." I sat across the table. "What are you reading?"

"*What to Expect When You're Expecting*. Amy suggested it." Abbie popped the remaining bite of whole-wheat toast into her mouth. "It's terrifying. I didn't know I should be so nervous about so many things."

I smiled. "Maybe you shouldn't read it then."

"If I stop reading, I'll think about Chris. I don't want to do that." She kept her eyes on her book. "I assume from your silence he talked to you."

I took a sip of water. "He said you ended it."

"Of course I ended it. What option did I have?"

"He wants to be with you. He wants to help."

"I know," Abbie said, her voice small.

"Why not let him?"

She gave me a look. "You can't be serious. It would be so unfair to Chris. He's a nice guy. A great guy. Why should he be stuck with a pregnant girlfriend soon to become a teenage mother? No." Abbie shook her head, making her sloppy ponytail swing. "Not if I can prevent it. If Lance wants to be involved, fine, but not Chris."

"Have you told Lance yet?"

She shook her head again, this time softer. "Dad said he'd go over there with me tomorrow."

I reached for her hand and squeezed it because someone should—Mom—and I was the only one available. "I think you're right about Chris."

Abbie's face beamed with gratitude. "Really?"

"Yeah. And no matter how Lance reacts or what he decides, you'll have me."

Then Dad barged through the garage door, grocery bags hanging from his arms. "Guess who has great news?"

"Uh, you?" I said.

Dad winked at me. "I always knew you were smart."

"So what's the good news?" Abbie asked.

"The Rosses are coming over for lunch." Dad grinned at us. "Isn't that great? I'm grilling salmon." As he realized we weren't celebrating, Dad looked up from unloading groceries. "What's wrong?"

"Nothing," I forced myself to say. "When do they arrive?"

"Not 'til 12:30. Plenty of time for you girls to get showered and come help."

Abbie gathered her book to her chest. "I'll go first." She shuffled out of the room.

Dad raised an eyebrow at me. "Did I do something?"

"No." I spun my water glass in quarter turns over and over. "She and Chris are sorting stuff out."

"Oh," Dad said.

During their phone conversation earlier in the week, Brian had apparently informed Dad of Chris and Abbie's relationship. If it upset Dad, he didn't say so.

Dad turned an inquisitive eye my direction. "What about you? You don't seem too thrilled either. I thought you and Connor got along these days."

I laughed. "Boy, do we."

I cringed, but Dad laughed. "Well, that sounds suspiciously like a crush to me. What happened to Eli?"

I searched for a concise answer. "I met Connor."

"And things are starting up with you guys?"

"It's nothing."

Dad took the chair beside me. "I don't think it works that way, kiddo."

"What do you mean?"

"Remember what I said to Abbie last night? We're going to be a family who works things out together. You don't get to pick and choose when that happens."

I squirmed in my seat. "But, Dad, it's boy stuff."

"You're in luck. Boy stuff is my expertise." He wiggled his eyebrows.

I laughed and bit my lower lip. "You sure?"

"Lay it on me."

"Okay." I folded my arms on top of the table. "Connor told me he loves me."

Although he tried to keep his face neutral, Dad's eyes widened. "When?"

"Last night."

"What did you say?"

"I didn't know what to say."

"Do you love him?"

I took a drink of water so I could swallow the lump in my throat. "Enough to know I'm no good for him."

Dad frowned. "Skylar, honey, what are you talking about? You're wonderful."

"I'm not, Daddy." My lip quivered and I bit it steady. "You just think that because I'm so much like Mom and you're in love with her."

Dad's head cocked as if he didn't understand. "You're not like your mom."

I laughed. "Yes I am. Everybody says so. *You* say so."

"You may look like her, but you don't act a thing like her."

"Are you crazy? I act *exactly* like Mom. I'm calm, rational, materialistic, and demand perfection of everybody around me."

"You know who that sounds like to me?" Dad asked. When I shook my head, he smiled. "Me."

"You?"

He nodded. "To a T."

"I'm like you?"

"Sorry, kiddo, but it's the truth. Even your mom thought so. Especially these last couple weeks as you've been figuring out how to sew. Whenever you threw out one of your projects because it wasn't perfect, she'd say to me, 'She's *your* daughter.' And"—he tapped his finger against my nose—"much like me, you'll find you can't give up on being with the person you love."

I knit my fingers together. "So you think I should give this thing with Connor a chance."

He nodded. "Your mom and I may have passed down traits to you, Skylar, but ultimately you're your own person. Our mistakes don't have to become your mistakes."

I considered this. "Are you going to keep trying with Mom?"

"Always." A crease developed between his eyes, just like me when I was on the brink of tears. "I thought maybe you, Abbie, and I could start counseling. Hopefully your mom will join us."

I squirmed at the thought of answering all those personal questions. "Why do Abbie and I need to go?"

"We have a lot of lost time to make up for. When I think back on the last couple years, all I really remember is work." He shook his head, his expression saggy with sadness. "I thought I was doing the right thing by working so hard. I always told myself that this was just until I could afford to slow down, but that time never really came. And look at you." He sighed as he evaluated my face. "You're not my little girl anymore. You're starting college in the fall."

"I'm still here, Dad," I said, reaching to hug him. "We have lots of time."

It was a tough call, who of Connor, Chris, Abbie, and me was most uncomfortable. Luckily, the adults were too engrossed in their own boring conversation to pay much attention to our lack thereof.

"Skylar, what are you going to be for Halloween?" Cameron asked, nearly bouncing in his seat. These days, nothing occupied his mind but costumes, monsters, and candy.

"I'm not dressing up."

Cameron looked at me with horror. "Why not?"

"I'm not trick-or-treating or going to any parties. There's no point."

"Mom!" he squawked. "Did you hear that?"

Amy turned an attentive ear to her son. "Hear what, dear?"

"Skylar isn't dressing up for Halloween!"

She smiled. "Sometimes that happens when you get older. Connor isn't dressing up this year either."

Connor and I glanced at each other. I offered him the best smile I could muster, but he looked away.

Cameron speared his baked potato with passion. "I will *always* dress up."

I continued looking at Connor, hoping he would look back. Nothing.

And so went the rest of lunch.

How was I supposed to do this, I wondered as I helped clear the table. I'd never approached a guy before about feelings. They'd always clobbered me with theirs before I got the chance.

Connor leaned close as I stacked plates. "Mind if we talk in private?"

That was a good start. "Sure," I said. "Come on."

He followed me to my bedroom. I instantly regretted bringing him there. I knew from years of living with my mom what all you could tell from someone's room. What would Connor think of my canopy bed with sheer white drapes? "A princess bed," Dad had said last year when it was delivered. Is that what it would look like to Connor too? Would it remind him of all those reasons he didn't want to be with me in the first place?

Connor burst out laughing. "How do you have a real conversation on this?" He picked up my pink, furry phone. "It's like a toy."

I didn't answer, just continued to watch him poke about my room. He seemed in no hurry to discuss whatever it was that required us being alone. Probably how we should forget all that stuff he said last night and just be friends. I wrung my hands. What should I say if he said that? Should I tell him I'd had a change of heart? That Dad had given me the green light to date him?

Connor peered at the single framed picture in my room, one of Abbie and me. In the picture we're five and three, dressed to impress in Mom's cocktail dresses. I remembered how Mom bent over me and brushed my face with powder. I loved how soft it was on my face, how it tickled my nose, how it made me smell like her. We used to have fun together.

"You guys look hilarious." Connor glanced at me. "Am I making you uncomfortable being in here?"

"No." Ugh—I was trying not to lie anymore. "Well, kind of. I've never had a boy in my room before."

Connor returned the photo to my dresser. "I'm honored."

I smiled, and then we just stood there.

"I want you to listen to me." He gripped my arms, holding me there as if I were a flight risk. "You don't get to drive off and pretend that settles everything. I know you care about me, and I refuse to give up based on some lame excuse about your mother. To you, I realize, it may seem legitimate, but I've seen a different side of you this week, a strong side, and there's not a doubt in my mind that—"

I cut him off by pressing my mouth to his. He drew me closer and his grip on my arms loosened as I relaxed against him.

Connor blushed as he looked into my eyes. "Really? I had this whole spiel planned."

With his grin and red cheeks, he looked like a little boy, but in a nice way. I pushed my fingers through his auburn waves. "Sorry."

Connor shrugged. "I'll save it for our first fight."

"Oh good. Something to look forward to."

Connor smiled and pulled me against him. "We have a lot to look forward to."

24

The dreaded Monday came quickly, as all dreaded days do. Though with Connor to walk beside me, it didn't seem so horrible. Heather was right when she said people ultimately would prove to be human, but life was sure better when they were around. And even when they disappointed, God wouldn't. Or so I was learning.

Chris and Abbie walked beside us, carrying on a noticeably strained conversation. Their subjects were too polite, their word choices too careful. With Lance's apparent eagerness to help with the coming child, I imagined it would be awhile before things between Chris and Abbie returned to normal. Assuming they could.

"Hey, Abbie, wait up!"

All four of us turned and saw Lance jogging our way. I caught the flash of jealousy in Chris's eyes before he could mask it.

"It's just not fair," I hissed to Connor. "Lance treated her like dirt when they were together, and now Chris has to lose to him?"

Connor pressed soothing fingertips into the nape of my neck. "There's a lot of time between now and the baby's arrival. A lot could still change."

"Well, say something encouraging to your brother. He looks horrible."

"I can hear you, you know," Chris said in a glum voice.

I glanced at Lance and Abbie, who'd fallen behind us. "You still matter to her," I said. "And Lance isn't exactly known for his follow-through."

Chris shrugged and veered off toward the sophomore hall.

"That was nice of you," Connor said as he wove his fingers through mine.

"I feel sorry for him." I shook my head. "Only Abbie would get pregnant and have two guys fighting to take care of her."

When we arrived at our lockers, Jodi and the rest of the girls were already there. Jodi noted Connor's and my joined hands. I assumed that in a matter of seconds I'd be wearing whatever her Starbucks cup contained.

Instead, she rolled her eyes. "I know you're miffed about Eli, but you don't have to stoop *that* low."

If she'd said something derogatory about me, that would be one thing. Messing with Connor was something else altogether. Maybe she knew that.

"Watch it, Jodi," I said.

Connor touched my arm. "It's not worth it."

"Listen to your boyfriend, Skylar." Jodi strolled past us, the other girls in tow. "Nice pants, by the way."

I waited until they were out of earshot to say, "I can't handle another seven months of them." When Connor didn't respond, I glanced at him. "Hello?"

He shook his head. "Sorry. I was focused on your pants. Exactly what color is that?"

I gave his arm a playful punch. "Thought you said you liked my crazy clothes."

"I love your crazy clothes." He pulled me close and kissed my forehead. "Although I'll admit they kept me at bay for a while."

"Well, same to you."

"Same to me?" Connor looked down at his wind pants and sneakers. "There's nothing wrong with my clothes."

"Hmm, I feel our first fight coming on."

He checked his watch. "Forty-eight hours. Yeah, that sounds about right."

"How about instead of arguing about your clothes, we take a moment to appreciate that I've learned to care about other things. And that you stuck with me through the messy ride."

"You were worth it," Connor said, fitting his arm around my waist. "You're not like any girl I've ever known."

A long time ago, I'd let Aaron hypnotize me with this idea, that I was somehow better than the girls around me. I craved distinction, uniqueness. My quest for my true identity led to that horrid night, the one I still had nightmares about.

"Do you think it's possible to get over big stuff in life?" I asked as we headed toward class. "Like do you think I'll ever forget what happened with Aaron and really move on?"

Connor drew in a slow breath. "I hope this comes out right. While I hate the thought of anything causing you pain, have you ever considered what might have happened if you hadn't met Aaron?"

"No."

"Think about it for a minute."

I did. A dark life lay ahead of that girl, full of hangovers and superficial relationships. I much preferred what I had now, my life after I got over myself.

"You know, maybe that's why we're not allowed do-overs," I said. "The events we'd erase, God uses to shape our lives."

Connor looked at me with pride. "I like how your life is shaping up."

I smiled. "Yeah, me too."

Dr. Prentice flipped on her tape recorder. "How's the week gone?" Her eyes rested on Dad, then Abbie, then me.

For the last month, we'd sat in the same chairs every Wednesday night at eight while she probed us about our communication, Dad's work schedule, and any contact with Mom. We were making progress, or so she claimed.

Abbie beamed at Dad. "Dad took the whole weekend off."

Dr. Prentice smiled. "Wonderful, Paul. And is it getting easier to delegate responsibilities at work?"

"It is. Like yesterday, this meeting came up that—" Dad stopped talking when the office door cracked open. He stood. "Teri."

I blinked at my mom as she stood in the doorway of Dr. Prentice's office, and searched for any changes the last month might have inflicted. But she looked the same as always—a smart outfit, just the right amount of makeup. Did we look the same to her? Or could she see all the tiny changes that had taken place in the weeks of her absence?

Mom glanced around the room, left eye twitching ever so slightly. "I'm sorry I'm late. I meant to come earlier, but . . ." Her words trailed off, and for a moment, she and my father looked at each other.

He pulled out a chair for her. "You're right on time," he said. "We're just getting started."

Acknowledgments

Over the course of several years as I wrote this book, many people influenced its creation.

First, my husband, Ben, who took lots of walks with me around Westwood while he helped me figure out exactly who Skylar was. He read every draft of this book along the way and was critical to the accuracy of my baseball and tire-changing scenes. He also indulged several research trips to Sheridan's.

My family and babysitters, without whom I wouldn't have time or energy to sit at my desk every day—Steve and Beth Hines, Reta Hines, and Ann and Bruce Morrill. And Chris Morrill, whom I draw my brotherly experiences from.

McKenna Noelle made it possible for me to write pregnancy with authority and prompted a major rewrite of Abbie's story.

The beautiful character of Amy Ross is a composite of the fabulous ladies who used to gather with me on Wednesday mornings back in Orlando—particularly Christy Kirven, Amy Etchison, Lucretia Head, Jan Cochran, Tricia Phillips, Julie Leffler, Deidre Anderson, and Elaine Gallman.

I'm indebted to Erica Vetsch, my first writing friend, who suggested I join ACFW. She's been here to encourage me every step of the way.

My three writing buddies—Mary Proctor, Carole Brown, and Roseanna White—who've made the journey so much more fun than when I wrote all by myself. Particularly Roseanna, a "kindred spirit" whose opinion I'm addicted to, and who makes sure I get all my commas and periods in the right places.

My agent, Kelly Mortimer. She consistently goes above and beyond her professional duties. Kelly pushes me to do my best and represents me and my stories with fervor and energy. She's living proof of how rich the rewards are when you obey God's calling for your life.

And of course the whole team at Revell. Their enthusiasm for Skylar's story has made it easy for Skylar to belong to everyone, not just me. Specifically Jennifer Leep, a champion for this series, and Jessica Miles, whose attention to detail touched my heart.

Thank you all for your invaluable help in making this book possible.

Stephanie Morrill is a twentysomething living in Overland Park, Kansas, with her high school sweetheart-turned-husband and their young daughter. She loves writing for teenagers because her high school years greatly impacted her adult life. That, and it's an excuse to keep playing her music really, really loud.